To truckers everywnere.

Many times we have seen a big rig pulled over and the driver changing a flat tire for someone or helping injured victims of an unfortunate accident. Thank you for being out there for the rest of us.

In the 1940s my mother and I were traveling west in a Studebaker convertible. My father had just come back from China and we were going to San Diego to meet his ship as it docked. It was late at night or sometime in the very early morning somewhere in New Mexico on route 66, a freak snowstorm had covered the road and mother had pulled over to the side unable to tell where the road was. Lights from a large truck pulled up behind us and a man knocked on mother's window. She rolled the window down and the man asked if we were in trouble. Mother explained she was unable to see the road and the driver made a comment something like this. "There's a town up here a ways and I'm going on through, you put this car in my tracks and keep my taillights in site. Don't get to close now or you and that boy there may end up someplace in heaven". My mother thanked him and said he was an angel. I will never forget his response. "No ma'am, I'm just a trucker". We made it through thanks to that trucker and I believe mother paid a whole three dollars for a motel room. I was seven or eight then. Until the day she died mother referred to all truckers as road angels. Hence, the book *Angry Angel* and the truck *Heaven Bound.*

Angry Angel

"I hate you! I hate all of you"! Angela screamed as she reached for her walking stick, found it, and then got up off the ground for the third time that morning. With tears streaming down her face, Angela felt her way along the path toward home. Her anger made her hurry and before long she fell again, this time skinning her knee. So, for the fourth time this morning, Angela had fallen. The laughter of the other children had done nothing to help her spirits either. She just knew they were laughing at her. In her anger she wished they would be struck blind. Then they would know how it feels to fall and be laughed at. That would teach them. Turning, she screamed back at her childhood friends, "I hate you! I hope all of you go blind"!

Her long-time childhood friend, Marsha, ran to her side and attempted to calm her. "Angie, you don't mean that. Surely, you don't want all of your friends to be blind". Marsha had taken hold of Angela's arm as she always did to help her along, but this time Angela knocked her hand away and turned to face her best friend. "Oh yes I do, Marsha, you're just like the rest of them. Always laughing at me when I fall. I hate you, too. I want you all to be blind like me and then you will know how it feels. Leave me alone. I'm going home. At least there I can talk to grandma and not fall all of the time".

Marsha stopped and watched as her childhood friend used her walking stick to feel her way along the path toward home. Now Marsha had tears in her own eyes. She called after Angela, "I love you Angela. It makes no difference to me if you can see or not. You're my best friend and I love you". As Marsha walked back to the other children, she cried quietly for her friend. It was not Angela's fault she had been born blind. Thinking how beautiful Angela was, Marsha shook her head in sorrow. For her friend would never know of her great beauty. She would never see the long brown curls that her grandmother fixed for her each day. She would never enjoy the hand-sewn dresses that she wore. "How sad," Marsha thought. "To be so beautiful and loved and yet so very angry all of the time. How very sad".

Arriving home, Angela found the door wouldn't open as it usually did. In anger she beat on it with her walking stick. "Grandmother, open the door"! She screamed, "Open the door"!

Grandmother Leslie was in the kitchen baking and didn't hear Angela at first. When she heard the banging and screaming she rushed to the door. Opening it, she found Angela sitting on the porch crying. "My word Angie, what is wrong with you. You know better than to do something like that. What will your grandfather say about all of these marks you have put on our door? Get up and come inside and quit that crying".

Angela jumped up and screamed again, "Everyone hates me, because I'm blind and different than they are! Well I hate all of you. I don't care about the door, or you, or grandfather either. He can just fix the old door. I'm leaving and never coming back. Then you won't have to bother with me ever again".

Whirling around in anger, and swinging her walking stick, she accidentally struck Grandmother Leslie on the side of the head, cutting her cheek and making her fall to the porch. Lying there dazed and confused all she could see was Angela starting down the steps and heading for the busy well-traveled road that ran in front of Grandfather Leslie's fields. Grandmother Leslie reached out and tried to speak to Angela, "Angie, Angie. Not into the road, please. It's dan...". Grandmother wasn't able to finish because the pain in her head made her faint.

Reaching the busy road, Angela carefully stepped up, stood on the edge and listened as the speeding traffic passed within inches of where she was standing. The wind made by passing cars and trucks dried the tears on her face. One motorist passed and honked for her to move back, she jumped and almost fell once again. The sound of a big truck slowing down and the hiss of air brakes as it came to a stop beside her frightened her even more.

"Say, sis, you're a bit young to be standing out here trying to get a ride aren't you? Where are you headed anyway"?

This was happening very fast, and Angela was caught off guard. She stammered, but only for a second. "I, I'm going to New York to see my Aunt Mazie. Do you suppose I might get a ride with you"? She said smiling up at the big round-faced driver.

"Well sis, I'm surely not going that far, but I reckon I can take you within a few hundred miles of there. Hop in, I got the road blocked here. Need to get movin' if I want to get my load delivered on time".

Angela stepped forward and ran into the step that led to the cab of the big truck. Grabbing hold, she pulled herself up, shut the door, and settled into the seat beside the driver. "Thank you mister, I have been standing there for a long while. My, isn't this one of those big trucks that I hear going by all the time"?

The driver watched her climb into the cab and was now sitting with his mouth open staring at her.

"Why, sis, ain't you blind"?

"Yes I am. Is that a problem for you? If it is, I will get out and find another ride. Of course you seem rather nice and I would rather ride with you, but I don't want to be a bother".

"No, no, sis. That's okay, but it does seem strange that a youngster like you would be out here on the busy road all by herself. Don't you have any kin to take care of you? I mean this is a shame, sis".

"I'll be fine," Angela replied. "Actually, I do this every year. Perhaps we had better get started before a policeman comes along and gives us a ticket for blocking this road".

The big man nodded his head. "You may be right, sis, and this is a big truck like you said. We have been together for a spell, too. Her name is Heaven Bound". The gears of the truck ground into place, and they started off, leaving Grandmother Leslie lying on the porch unconscious.

Two

Angela sat quietly for a long time wondering if grandmother would miss her. Her Aunt Mazie would be glad to see her, but it had been two years since she had been back for a visit to the farm. Aunt Mazie was grandmother's older sister, and both, she and grandmother had grown up on the farm. Married to a young doctor by the name of Richard Carter, she had moved to New York many years ago. Angela didn't know exactly where she lived in New York, but it couldn't be too hard to find her. She had heard people ask grandmother where different people lived in their town of Rockville. She decided she would just do that when the time came.

Angela was awakened by the driver, who was gently pulling on her arm. "Sis, hey sis. You best be wakin' up. It's about dinnertime. Ain't you hungry? We got a ways to go, better have a bite to eat, don't you think"? The big truck pulled into the diner and made a loud hissing sound as the driver took his foot off the brake and turned off the engine. "You just sit tight, sis. I'll come around and help you down. That seat is pretty high up and ain't no need of you fallin' and getting all skinned up before you see your aunt.

This was exactly the kind of thing Angela didn't like and she got mad all over again. People were always thinking she couldn't do things for herself. Well, it was time to start right now. "No thank you, Mr. Driver, I can do it by myself. I am twelve years old". The big man shrugged his shoulders and watched as she opened the door, stepped out and promptly fell to the ground. Leaping out himself, he rushed around the front of the truck to find Angela sitting on her backside with tears running down her cheeks and her hat hanging on the side of her head. She wasn't hurt, but she sure was one mad, little girl!

Reaching down, the big man helped her to her feet and stepped back. Taking his cap off, he stood looking at her, scratching his head. "You know, sis, it ain't a bad thing to have some help now and then. We all need it at some time or another. It ain't your fault you can't see, but on the other hand it ain't our fault either. Now, if you will give me your hand, we will go on in to Gus's' diner here and have us some dinner. Reaching down, the big man took hold of Angela's hand and together they started across the parking lot toward the diner. A strange sight, this huge man and the tiny little girl walking hand in hand. Taking his red bandana out of his pocket and putting it in her hand he said, "Better wipe your tears and blow your nose, sis, don't want these truckers to think you been cryin' or nothin' like that. Maybe somebody smaller, but not nobody as big as you".

Angela heard the bell ring as the big man opened the diner door and still holding her hand helped her inside. The waitress looked up and smiled, "Howdy Ben, you always seem to know when we have meatloaf. Who's that you got with you? Slide into that booth there by the window and I'll be over in a minute".

He smiled and said, "I picked this here youngster up a few miles back. She's headed to New York to see her aunt. Thought I could help out some. Bring two of them plates of meatloaf, coffee for me and I guess milk for sissy here".

"New York! Why Ben, you don't go to New York. That's more than a thousand miles out of your way. Have you lost your mind? That outfit you're pulling for will fire you sure. I'll bring the meatloaf. You two go on and sit down".

After they were seated, Angela took off her hat and coat, folded it, and set it in the corner of the booth out of the way. For the first time, the big trucker had a chance to look at her. She was clean, and it was easy to see her dress had been made with great care. This was no ragamuffin runaway child. No, this little girl belonged somewhere and to somebody who loved her very much. The big man made a decision there and then. "Sis, if you will excuse me for just a minute, I got to do something. I'll be right back. Just you sit tight now".

"You're not going to leave me here are you mister? I need to get to my Aunt Mazie's. I suppose I could get a ride with one of these other nice people if you wanted to go on by yourself. I don't want to be a bother to anybody".

With a serious look, the big man leaned over so he could talk in Angela's ear without being overheard. "Now sis, I told you I would help you for as long as I could and I will do that. I just need to make a phone call and I will be right back. I promise".

Angela smiled, "I heard that lady call you Ben. Is that your name"?

"Yep, reckon it is at that. Benjamin, actually. That's my Christian name. Had it a good while, too".

Angela laughed for the first time that day, and stuck out her hand. "Well, Benjamin Actually, I'm glad to know you. My name is Angela, but you can call me sis if you want. I don't mind at all".

He took her hand in his and smiled down at this little blind girl. He turned to leave, but she wouldn't let go of his hand. "You have a very big hand, Benjamin. Are you a big man"?

Once again he smiled. "Well sis, I guess you could say that. Been big all my life I reckon. You best let go of my hand so I can make that call. Our dinner will be here in a minute".

Still holding his hand, Angela looked up at the big man. "Do you mind if I see what you look like Benjamin"?

"How do you do that with you bein' blind like you are"?

Again she smiled, "Well, you just lean over here and I will feel your face. That way I can see in my mind what you look like. It won't hurt, really".

Leaning over, the big man stood very still while Angela ran her hands over his face. His big nose and scratchy beard made her laugh. "Yes Benjamin, you are a very big man. You sure do have a big face, and you need to shave your beard. My grandpa shaves his beard every day".

By the time the big man returned, the food had already been delivered to the booth and Angela sat waiting. "Well, I see we're ready to eat". He slid into the booth being careful not to knock over Angela's glass of milk that had been set carefully in the middle of the table.

Reaching over, he picked up her knife and started to cut her food for her. "Here, sis, I'll just cut this stuff up a bit so you can get to it better".

"There is no need to do that, Benjamin. I can take care of myself very well," she said, as she touched his hand and pushed it away.

"Oh, I don't mind at all. It doesn't hurt for us to help those in need from time to time. We are supposed to do that anyway," Benjamin said, as he tried to continue. The tone of Angela's voice and the look on her face caused him to stop what he was doing. Angela's face had turned white with anger and her jaw was clamped shut so tight she had to speak through her teeth. "I told you I could take care of myself"! Getting louder with each word. "Why does everyone think I am so helpless"? By now she was screaming, "Just because I am blind doesn't mean I can't even eat by myself! You are just like all the rest! I hate you too"! Angela leaped up from the table and, with all the customers looking on, knocked her food off on the floor. She turned and started for where she thought the door should be and ran straight into the table next to where she and Benjamin had been sitting. Tripping over a chair, she fell to the floor and lay there sobbing with rage. The big man leaped up from his seat and reached down to help her up. "Leave me alone"! She screamed. "Just leave me alone"! The waitress had been watching and was instantly at Angela's side. "Ben, let me take care of this. I have three kids of my own. Give us a minute here". The big man nodded and returned to his seat. Unable to eat he just sat and watched as the waitress put her arms around the little blind girl and began to talk softly to her. After a while she helped Angela to her feet and together they headed to the washroom.

Wetting a clean washcloth with warm water, the waitress began to gently clean Angela's face. "Honey, my name's Flo. What in the world happened out there? You near scared poor ol' Ben to death. He's one of the nicest people you will ever meet, and he was just trying to help. Most folks wouldn't even waste their time. While

I'm thinking about it, what are you doing with Ben anyway? Seems to me you are a long way from home".

"Hi, Flo. My name is Angela, and I'm on my way to see my Aunt Mazie in New York. Ben has agreed to take me as far as he can. Once I get there I will just ask someone where my Aunt Mazie lives. I do that every year you know. Most everyone there knows her. My uncle Robert was a doctor before he died a few years ago and she used to help him in the office. So, everyone knows her".

Flo stood listening to Angela in amazement. New York was one of the biggest cities in the world. It was obvious this little girl had never been there. "Your Aunt Mazie, Angela, what would her last name be? I've been to New York a time or two and I don't think I have ever met her".

"That is very strange alright. Most people have met her at one time or another. Her name is Mazie Carter, wife of Doctor Richard Carter. Do you think we should go back out and let Ben know I am all right? He will probably be worried. You are right about him; he is a very nice man. And I am hungry. Besides I want to tell him I am sorry for the way I acted".

"Good idea. Here, let's straighten your dress and we will go back out there just like nothing happened. We girls must stick together you know". Flo straightened Angela's dress and together they walked back to the booth where Benjamin was still seated. He hadn't touched a bite of his food and was relieved to see Angela had calmed down and was her old self again. She slid into the booth across from him and looked up. "Benjamin, I am sorry for the way I treated you just now. Sometimes it is very hard for me to allow others to help me. Please forgive me".

The big man smiled and picked up his fork. "Think nothing of it sis. Why, I get upset myself from time to time. Now we better eat our lunch, we got us a ways to go if we are going to see your Aunt Mazie".

Flo had been standing quietly by the table listening to the conversation. "I'm going to get you two some hot food. After all that has just happened your meal is cold". She picked up the plates and disappeared into the kitchen returning shortly with clean plates filled with meatloaf, mashed potatoes, gravy and green beans. "There now, suppose you two get busy and clean those up. I don't like to see my meatloaf go to waste".

They finished eating, and after Benjamin paid he and Angela started for the door. "We got us a ways to go tonight, best get that big rig on the road".

At the end of the room, near the door, sat three men who had been watching things unfold for the last half hour. As Angela and the big man approached the door the three stood up and blocked their way. The leader of the three was a large bearded man. Stepping forward, he looked Benjamin square in the face. "Mister, we been watching you for the last half hour, and I don't reckon you need to be leaving with that child there. You just step away and leave her to us. We'll see she gets home all right".

The big man didn't move anything but his head. He looked first at the bearded man and then at the other two. He then turned and gently picked up Angela, opened the screen door of the café and set her outside. "You just wait here, child, this will just take a minute, and then we'll be on our way".

Angela smiled and squeezed his hand. "Benjamin, please be careful. I don't want anything bad to happen to you".

The big man laughed heartily and patted her on the shoulder. "Not to worry, sis. Everything is going to be just fine". He turned and stepped back through the door and stood directly in front of the three men once again. The broad smile and white teeth failed to hide the hardness of his eyes. Clinching his massive fists he placed them on his hips and looked into the eyes of the large bearded man. "Men, this here child and I have business that is none of your concern. You would do well to just sit back down there and finish your pie and leave us be. If you feel you need to carry this any further please do it now. I ain't got the time to mess with you much longer".

The three looked at this giant standing before them and sat back down to finish their pie. Benjamin said good-bye to Flo and walked back through the door. Taking Angela's hand he started for the truck. "Well, Sis, that didn't take too much time did it"?

Angela stopped long enough to put her hat back on then looked up and smiled, "Nope, didn't take long at all. How far do we have to go to get to New York, Benjamin? I am anxious to see my aunt. She said the last time she was home that she would be looking for me".

"Well, sis, we got us a ways to go all right. Something over nine hundred miles I reckon. If we drive steady and sleep just a little bit we should make it there sometime tomorrow. We better get this old girl started and on the road. When she gets to humming the miles will just fade away under them big wheels of hers". Opening the door, he lifted Angela up and sat her on the passenger seat. "Sis, you be sure and buckle up now. Don't want anything to happen to you before we get you to your aunt's place. You do know where she lives in New York, don't you"?

"Oh yes, Benjamin, I have been there many times when I was little. It has been a while since I have seen Aunt Mazie, but I do know about where she lives. Its right after you cross over this big bridge and go just a short distance. As soon as we do that I will ask someone and we will be there in a jiffy. My uncle was a doctor and everyone knew them. You will like Aunt Mazie, Benjamin. She is very nice".

Three

The big rig rolled northeast towards Pennsylvania and the skies began to darken with the approach of a summer storm. No matter, Ben had been driving for years in all kinds of weather and it didn't bother him. Back at the truck stop he had done something that he hadn't mentioned to Angela, and had never done before. When he had excused himself from the table he made a phone call to the company he had been hauling for and told them he had an emergency, and was dropping their trailer where it was. They would need to send another tractor and pick it up for its final destination run. The dispatcher was a longtime friend of Ben's and said he would take care of it. He told Ben that he was to check in upon his return for another load. Ben thanked his friend and returned to the table. So now the two travelers were riding along in a tractor without a trailer. It was a little bumpy, but Angela didn't seem to notice. Thunder rolled across the Ohio sky, and Ben looked over at Angela to find her curled up asleep on the big seat with her coat wrapped around her.

Lightning crashed around them waking Angela up for a second, but the hum of the big truck's engine put her back to sleep. They were now in Pennsylvania working their way north and closer to New York. Ben had an uneasy feeling about this little girl he had befriended. She seemed not to be afraid, but at the same time not at all sure of where she was going. New York was a town of several million people, and if she wasn't right about her directions she might not be able to find her Aunt Mazie at all. The thought of this little blind girl alone on the streets of New York made the big man nervous. Lightning crashed again and this time she woke up hungry. "Benjamin, do you think we might get something to eat? It has been a long time since our lunch with Flo, and I am very hungry".

The big man smiled at the little blind girl then realized that she couldn't see him. Strange, he thought to himself. This little child is so normal in every way, except for her terrible temper of course. She just can't see. "Sure, sis. We'll stop just as soon as we can. There is a truck stop up here a ways. We'll pull off there. Just you go on back to sleep and I'll wake you when we get there".

Skillfully guiding the big rig on through the night and the storm, as he had so many times in the past, Ben thought about how he was going to help this little girl find her aunt in a city the size of New York. Thunder rolled again and lightning flashed giving the Pennsylvania countryside an eerie glow. Slowly, the blackness of night began to give way to thin strip of light that began to show in the eastern sky. The big man found he was fighting sleep and knew it was time to pull the big rig over. Pulling into one of the truck stops along highway 80, he eased it into one of the slips and shut the big diesel down. Angela was still curled up in the passenger seat next to him, and he decided not to crawl in the sleeper behind the driver's seat. He leaned his massive body back against the seat and closed his eyes. His last thought before drifting off to sleep was how fresh and clean the air always smelled after a rain. How sweet the air smelled coming through the open window. "Thank you, God, for cleaning things up a bit. These big old diesels do get things a might dirty, and I do need your help with this child here. The truth would be much appreciated".

The sun was full up when Ben woke to the sound of Angela's voice ringing in his ears. She was talking rather excitedly and pulling on his shirtsleeve. "Benjamin, why are we stopped like this? Is something wrong with the truck? Are you sick? Where are we"? Shaking his head to clear it from sleep he sat up in the seat and stretched. "Easy there sis, I'll be with you in a minute".

She became more excited, "What do you mean you will be with me in a minute? You know I am on my way to see my Aunt Mazie. She is waiting on me," she screamed, hitting him on the arm "I hate you. You are just like all the rest! I hate you"! She said, slamming herself back down into the seat.

Ben was surprised by her outburst and sat there a minute before he spoke. "Now you just hold on there a minute, sis".

Angela broke in again screaming at him, "Sis! I am not your sis! My name is Angela. I was named after the angels. So don't call me sis. I am not your sis"!

He muttered something about angels under his breath and continued, "I am the one driving this rig and I can't go on forever without sleep. You are sleeping aren't you? Have been most of the night, except when you asked for something to eat. If I don't get some sleep from time to time neither one of us will get to where we're going. This big rig of mine will be heaven bound for sure. Not a bad thought, but the time ain't right just now. Least, I hope it's not". He could see by the expression on her face that his words were not calming her down a bit. In fact she was even angrier than before.

"Heaven bound"! She screamed. "I want to go to New York City and be with my Aunt Mazie. Oh! I do hate you so. You are just like all the rest of them. I don't need you or your heaven-bound truck. What a stupid thing to say. I don't want you to do anything for me. I don't need your help at all. I can find my own way"!

To Ben's amazement she opened the door and jumped out. On most big rigs it is something over five feet from the seat to the ground and this one was no different.

"Lord help me with this child," he said as he opened his own door and leaped out. Running around to the front of the truck, he was again amazed to see that Angela had landed on her feet and was running wildly across the truck stop parking lot. The further she got the more hissing of brakes and blowing of air horns he could hear. He watched in horror as she darted directly into the path of the outbound trucks that were continuing on their way after a night's rest in the truck stop. He also knew that if this kept up she would be hit for sure, and he began to run after her. Faster and faster he ran watching helplessly as she ran directly toward a huge rig that was picking up speed in the outbound lane. Ben could see that the driver couldn't see her. She was far too small, and the truck was much too close. He was winded, but tried to scream anyway, "Angela, run to the side honey. Run to the side"! It was no use, she couldn't hear him. The big diesel was too loud. Ben was running as fast as he could, but he knew there was no chance he would be in time. "God, help her"! He screamed. "She can't see. She can't see"! The big man stopped gasping for air and fell to his knees in tears watching helplessly as the big rig bore down on her.

Of course Angela had no way of knowing, but she was just inches away from being hit by the large truck. Benjamin was still on his knees watching out of tear-filled eyes when a pair of very strong hands grabbed hold of Angela's coat and jerked her from the very jaws of certain death. She felt herself being lifted and pulled rather roughly to one side. With a yelp she struck out at the very hands that had just saved her life. "Benjamin! You take your hands off me this very minute. If you don't want to help me, I will just find someone who will".

When Ben saw what had happened he got to his feet and hurried over to where she was now standing. Seeing an old friend standing by Angela, he knew his prayer had been answered. "Thank you Father," he whispered under his breath. The broad smile of the man who was just now setting Angela down was a familiar one, but one Benjamin hadn't seen in quite some time. Thankful Angela was safe, he shook his old friend's hand. "Thank you, Abraham, I owe you".

"Think nothing of it, Ben. Didn't look like you were going to get here in time. By the way, were my eyes deceiving me, or did I just see my old friend Benjamin Mansfield drop to his knees in front of God and everybody right out here in the open? Got to confess old friend, I didn't think I would ever see that day come for you. Proud of you boy, but next time you might wait to do it until the business at hand is taken care of".

Unaware of the danger she had been rescued from, Angela was curious as to whom Ben was speaking with. "Benjamin, who is this man, and why did you grab my coat so roughly? You almost made me fall". Sticking out her hand, Angela introduced herself, "How do you do, sir, my name is Angela. I am going to New York to visit my Aunt Mazie, and Benjamin has agreed to give me a ride as long as he is going that way".

Abraham shook her hand and introduced himself, "How do you do, young lady. My name is Abraham Morris. It is a pleasure to meet you. My old friend Benjamin here often helps folks in distress". Seeing the little girl was blind, he looked at Benjamin and spread his hands. Leaning over he whispered in Ben's ear. "Are you out of your mind Ben? What in the name of heaven are you doing with this child"? Getting more excited with every breath, Abraham begin speaking louder, "I'll tell you one thing right now! You better get this child in your truck and get her back to where she came from and I mean right now"! Where is your truck anyway"? Looking around he spotted Heaven Bound sitting about fifty feet away. He stood looking at her for a moment and then turned back to Ben. "Where's the trailer? The trailer is gone Ben. The trailer is gone for Pete's sake! THE TRAILER'S GONE"!

Angela interrupted them, "What does he mean, the trailer's gone? What did you do with the trailer Ben? I thought you had a delivery to make in New York. How can you possibly make a delivery if you have no trailer? What's going on Benjamin"?

Abraham was nodding his head in agreement. "Uh huh. You see there. How can you make a delivery if you have no trailer? And what are you doing going to New York anyway. Your run is to Chicago, has been for years. You having some kind of breakdown or something you ain't talking about? Out here in the middle of nowhere with this child and no trailer. You have always been strange boy, but this takes the cake. You beat all I ever seen. You know that? I'll tell you what we better do". Abraham said, taking a few steps back out of the line of sight. "We better put this child on the next bus and get back to doing what we are supposed to be doing. Good Lord, listen to me. I ain't even in this. Look at all these folks standing around watching us. That's it for me old friend. I'm going in there and get me something to eat, and I'm out of here. You're plumb nuts". Abraham turned away and without looking back hurried into the restaurant.

"That sounds good to me too, Benjamin. I'm hungry. Let's eat. Mr. Abraham sounds very nice. Have you known him a long time"?

Ben took her hand and together they started for the restaurant. Looking around he could see what Abraham was talking about. There were indeed people watching this giant of a man walking along with this little girl. He stopped suddenly, startling her, "Angela, this ain't right. There are people watching you and me. I do want to help you, but you ain't my kin. Maybe Abraham was right at that. Maybe we should just take you back home and have this over with. I don't want any trouble".

Angela smiled and tugged on the big man's hand. "Don't worry, Benjamin, I'll just tell anyone who asks that you are my uncle, and we are going to New York together. That should take care of everything. Come on, I am starved".

Reluctantly, the big man moved forward and opened the door. Together they stepped inside, and when they did, all went quiet. The big man stood very still and looked around. About halfway back he spotted his friend Abraham sitting alone in a booth. Abraham was looking at them and very slightly shaking his head no. He even made a slight hand movement indicating he didn't want them to look at him. Without hesitation Angela tugged on Ben's hand and said, "Come on Uncle Benjamin. I'm hungry, let's eat". Ben forced a big smile and together they started toward the booth that Abraham occupied. Ben guided Angela into the seat and slid in beside her.

Abraham was beside himself. "Your mind is completely gone. I haven't seen you in two years and then one day here I am minding my own business and you show up just in time to get me killed.

You see the people sitting here? Do you? Let me tell you something about these people in here, Benjamin. These ain't ordinary folks my friend. No! These folks are truckers. You know what that means? I'm going to tell you what that means. That means they will do anything in the world for you if you're straight with them, but it also means, if you get on the wrong side of them, your family will never see you again. You will disappear from the face of the earth just like you were never born. Now I don't know about you..."

Angela interrupted Abraham in the middle of his sentence. "Uncle Abraham! Is that you? Uncle Benjamin, you didn't tell me we were going to meet Uncle Abraham here today". She opened her arms for a hug, and Abraham began sinking down into the seat. Benjamin gently pressed her arms down and suggested they order. Embarrassed, as they were, both were happy to see Angela's acting seemed to have quieted the rest of the folks in the restaurant.

When the food came, Abraham sat quietly eating for a while, and then looked up at his old friend. "You know you're into something here you shouldn't be into don't you"? He didn't wait for Ben to answer but continued, "This is like walking on a razor blade Ben. You do know that"? This time the big man nodded in agreement. Abraham continued, "You are going to take this child all the way to New York to meet her aunt. Is that right"? Again Ben nodded. "I've made quite a few runs up there. Where about in New York does she live"?

"New York City".

"Uh huh, but where"?

"Ain't sure exactly. We'll have to look for her when we get there. Angela says she will ask around".

Abraham's mouth fell open and he dropped his fork. Looking first at Angela, then back at Ben, then back at Angela again. Then he just collapsed back against the seat.

"Come on, Abe. It ain't all that bad. We got us a pretty good idea of about where it is".

"Oh yeah, and where is that"?

"Well, it's on one side or the other of the bridge that crosses the river".

Abraham sat staring at his old friend for a few seconds then said, "Ooookay. See you around Uncle Benjamin". He slid out of the booth and went to the register to pay his bill. Just before walking through the door, he looked back at Ben and shook his head.

"Did he leave"? Asked Angela.

"Yep, he's gone".

"That's a shame. He seemed so nice. A little nervous though, I had this feeling he didn't want to be here with us".

Ben nodded. "You know Angela, I sort of had that same feeling myself. Better finish your lunch. We have a ways to go if you want to see your Aunt Mazie anytime soon".

Four

Angela's grandfather had come in from the field shortly after
Angela had run away. Finding grandmother lying on the porch in a
daze, he became very concerned. She seemed to be all right, but
she was confused for a moment. Helping her to the porch swing,
he ran and brought a glass of water from the well and sat down
beside her, "What happened dear? Did you have another one of
your fainting spells? You know what the doctor told us about you
overdoing it. You must take it very slow if you are to get over this
virus".

Grandmother waved her hand impatiently. "No, Herbert, that's not
the reason. Angela accidentally hit me in the head with her walking
stick. Poor thing, she didn't even know she did it. She would feel
just terrible if she knew. Have you seen her? I thought perhaps
she might have come to the field to find you. When she gets
upset, you are the one she usually goes to".

"No. I saw her at breakfast of course, but not since then. She
could have gone to the barn though. You know how she loves the
animals, and it is a good place to pout. I'll go check".

Grandmother leaned back against the swing and closed her eyes
thinking of Angela. For some reason, it had been very hard for
Angela to adjust to being blind. She thought that strange because
everyone she had ever known that was blind had seemed to adjust
quite well. Not so with Angela, she had always fought blindness
like there was something that could be done about it. Maybe it was
because she was so full of energy. Hearing grandfather return,
she turned, half expecting to see Angie walking beside him. Not
seeing Angela caused her grave concern. "My word, Herbert,
where in the world could she have gone? She can't take care of
herself. Oh, Herb". Grandmother began to weep.

Grandfather put his arm around her shoulder to console her. "I
don't know, but we had better find out and pretty quick. If she
wandered off into the woods we might not find her for days, if at

all". Knowing he had said too much already, grandfather stopped talking and together they sat in silence thinking about their little Angela.

Grandmother was well aware of the dangers of the woods. She also knew how much worse it would be for someone without sight. A car coming up the long gravel drive interrupted their thoughts. When it pulled into the yard they could see it was Sheriff Wilson's car. The sheriff got out and walked toward the porch.

Grandmother and grandfather expected the worst. Sheriff Wilson was a rather small man, but all business. Taking off his hat, he looked briefly at the cut on grandmother's head and shook hands with them before speaking. "Afternoon Margaret, Herbert. That's a nasty cut you got on your head Margaret. How'd that happen anyway"?

Grandmother started to speak, but grandfather held up his hand stopping her. "Accident, Harley. What can we do for you"?

The sheriff nodded. "Don't think there is much to this folks, just came by to see if Angela is here"?

"No she isn't, Harley. We were just talking about that when you drove in. Seems she accidentally hit Margaret in the head with her walking stick and has gone off somewhere. I was just about to go to the woods and look for her".

Sheriff Wilson seemed nervous and ran his fingers through his thick black hair before continuing, "Folks, I don't mean to frighten you, but not more than an hour ago we received a call at the station about her. Seems someone saw a girl who looked a whole lot like Angela climbing into the cab of a tractor-trailer outfit. Grandmother moaned and covered her face with her hands in worry. Just then the radio in the sheriff's car crackled and they listened as the voice of the dispatcher confirmed that a girl fitting Angela's description was seen coming out of a trucker's diner in the northeast part of the state. "Herb, Margaret, I'll need to know what she was wearing when she left here"?

He was already speeding down the drive as he called in the information. With screeching tires and blaring siren, Sheriff Wilson pulled out onto the road leading to town. He called for the dispatcher to put out a statewide alert, and to call the sheriff in the next county to the north. They would need to quickly get the truck she was in stopped and arrest the driver for kidnapping. Angela was in serious trouble and it was a grim-faced law officer that was just now thinking of what might befall this beautiful little girl. It was between clenched teeth that he whispered, "Not on my watch. We lose no children on my watch".

Five

Ben and Angela climbed up into the big tractor and pulled out onto the highway. "Buckle up and get comfortable, sis. We got us a ways to go tonight. With any luck you will be seeing your aunt sometime tomorrow". Turning a couple of knobs on the CB he reached for the mike, "Breaker southbound," he said. "Break one time, for Heaven Bound". It wasn't but a second and the radio cracked back.

"Go ahead break, Dragon Slayer here. Is that you big Ben? You're a little off your usual run ain't you? What's up"?

"Yep, it's me. Got some personal business here. Need to make some time tonight and was wondering how the roads are between here and New York"?

"No problem that I've seen, Ben. A little construction work about a hundred miles back, but it was on the southbound lanes. You got clear roads all the way in. What kind of business you got anyway"?

Ben looked over and saw Angela was listening to his conversation with Dragon Slayer. "Nothin' special, Dragon Slayer. Going to see some of my relatives is all. Catch you later on down the line. Stay rubber side down brother. Heaven Bound is north bound and down".

"Same to you my friend. Dragon Slayer's big wheels are rollin' south".

Ben looked over at Angela again and found her smiling. "What's so funny, sis"?

"Oh nothing, Benjamin. Do all of you truckers talk like that"?

"Yep. Reckon so, sis. Sounds kind of funny don't it"?

"Well no. I kind of like it actually. Makes me feel like I'm part of something special".

Six

The big man smiled. "Welcome to the road, sis. There ain't nothin' in this world like truckin'. Oh it's hard work and there are times when we think we might like to have one of those regular jobs, but then the moon comes up and the night sky turns to velvet and it seems as if it is covered with beautiful diamonds for as far as the eye can see. Or the sun starts up and the sky turns all pink and beautiful and you know it is going to be a good day. Those are the times when you know you made the right choice about driving for a living".

Angela smiled, reached out and patted the big man's arm. "I'm glad I found you, Benjamin. I'm going to sleep if you don't mind. Do you think we will be in New York City tomorrow"?

"Count on it, sis. Might be there before the sun comes up. If we are, I'll wake you so you can see it clear the skyline". Realizing what he had said he quickly apologized. "Sorry sis. I didn't mean nothin' by that".

Angela clapped her hands together with glee. "No! No, Benjamin. It's all right. You have just treated me like I am a regular person. I like that very much".

"You are a regular person, sis. Why do you say that? Just because you can't see doesn't mean that you aren't a regular person".

"I know, Ben. It's just that all of my life people have been waiting on me and treating me differently than they would other people. I just want to be treated the same as everyone else is all".

The big man thought about that for a minute, then nodded. "Better grab that blanket behind the seat there, sis. Going to be a cold night. Gets that way up here in this north country". He watched as Angela searched around for the blanket. It would have been an easy matter for him to reach over, grab the blanket and hand it to her, but he let her find it for herself. He watched as she covered herself and closed her eyes. "Night, sis".

Her smile was barely visible in the darkness. "Night, Benjamin, and thank you for helping me".

The huge man had tears in his eyes as he looked out into the night sky. "Lord, help me help this child".

The hum of the big wheels put Angela to sleep and the lights from the dash of the big truck lit up the smile on Ben's face as they drove on into the darkness. Mile after mile the big rig's wheels ate up the road heading toward New York City. Beautiful Angela lay sleeping peacefully beside this giant of a man. She had no way of understanding there were millions and millions of people living in the city they were headed for. As Ben thought about the enormity of it he shook his head in wonderment. It was going to be something more than asking someone standing on a corner somewhere where her aunt lived. He didn't know how he was going to make it work for her, but he did know he was going to try. To turn this child over to the authorities in such a large city would frighten her indeed. He made up his mind right there and then that wasn't going to happen.

Dawn was breaking, and he was still winding his way through the high country when the crack of his CB startled him. "Hey, Heaven Bound. Is that you runnin' bobtail up there boy"?

Ben grinned and reached for the mike, "Well, my, my, I do believe I am hearing Uncle Abraham. I thought you were headed for Shaky Town. Whatever are you doing draggin' my tail, Desert Runner? You wouldn't be worried about ol' Ben would you"?

"And what if I am? You know you're in way over your head here. Heaven Bound or no, I figure you need help, boy. So I have decided to pass this load and tag along just to keep you out of trouble".

"You mean you are going to actually allow someone else to drive that raggedy rig of yours all the way from here to Shaky Town? Uncle Abraham, that is almost three thousand miles one way. You think that rig will make it that far without falling apart"?

All of the radio talk had awakened Angela, and when she recognized the voice on the other end of the radio she began to grin. Reaching over, she touched Ben's arm, "Tell Abraham I said hello Benjamin. I will be glad to see him again".

The big man grinned and patted her hand. "Okay sis, I'll tell him".

Abraham explained that he had made arrangements to pass his truck on to a trusted friend at a truck stop about fifty miles further on. His friend Woody Miller was to drive his truck on to San Francisco, make the delivery, and pick up another load that was waiting to be driven to Bangor, Maine. Abraham believed his business with Ben and Angela would be finished by then and could meet the man somewhere along the road and complete his run. The idea sounded good to Ben, and so he agreed to meet up with Abraham at the truck stop and then the three of them would continue on together.

Ben thought about this for a minute, and made a decision that seemed a good idea at the time. His tractor was somewhat newer than his friend Abraham's, and he felt the least he could do for his friend was to allow him to use his tractor to pull the load to San Francisco for his friend.

"Tell you what, Abraham. As long as you are willing to help your old friend. Suppose we switch tractors and we drive yours on in to New York. Woody can hook mine to the load and make the run out west and back. No offense, but my rig is newer than yours and we are pressed for time here. I don't want to leave you stranded somewhere and not know if Woody made it back all right. That sound about right to you"?

"That will do Benjamin. That will do just fine. By the way, how's Angela getting along"?

"She's fine. Says hi, and will be glad to see you". Benjamin felt strange using that language about Angela, but there wasn't any other way he knew how to put it. What do you say when speaking about a blind person? He decide the best thing to do was just be himself. Seemed easier all the way around.

Arriving at the truck stop just after eight in the morning, they waited while Abraham made the transfer of the tractors. Then the three of them entered the diner together to have breakfast before continuing on their journey. The three received some stares from the other customers, but this was a truck stop and truckers were used to seeing many different things. As long as they felt no one was in trouble or hurt in any way, they kept pretty much to themselves.

Taking a booth, they ordered and made small talk while waiting on their food. Angela was sitting beside Benjamin, and Abraham sat across from them. Looking at the two of them together he decided that he had done the right thing in offering his help. It was not that he didn't approve of what his friend was doing so much as how it looked to others. He knew from experience that outsiders though meaning well, could, and did for that matter, jump to the wrong conclusions without getting all the facts first. When that happened more often than not it led to real trouble. So now, here he sat right in the middle of it all. "Okay you two. What's the plan? Where do we go from here"?

Angela smiled and spoke right up. "Well, we go on into New York and ask where my aunt lives. When we find her you can just drop me off and be on your way".

Abraham looked at Benjamin, and the big man smiled. "Sounds simple enough to me, sis, but we could have a bit of a problem with that if we're not careful". Abraham winced when he heard Ben say this. He knew what was coming next, but knew also it had to be said. If this didn't work out, they would have to leave Angela with the authorities and neither one of them wanted to do that.

Seven

Sheriff Wilson put out the all-points bulletin for any rig that looked suspicious, but with so many rigs on the road he knew it would be extremely difficult, if not impossible for Angela to be found. He hadn't shared that information with Grandmother and Grandfather Leslie because he didn't want to frighten them. They were such good people, and it didn't seem to him it would serve any purpose to give them that kind of news at this time. It would be hard enough later on. He made a decision to call in the FBI. One of his deputy officers, Clint Sargent heard him make the call to Indianapolis and raised his eyebrows. "Holy mackerel Harley, this ain't all that serious is it? The girl most probably wandered off somewhere and will turn up shortly. She ain't been gone but a day. Seems to me we're getting a bit worked up here".

Sheriff Wilson finished his call and hung up the phone, "Clint, I know you mean well, but we got us a little blind girl out there somewhere on one of the interstates of this country heading who knows where, with who knows who, and she may well be in real trouble. Being blind, she can't tell where she is or how to get back here. She can't even run off and find a phone. Even if she could she wouldn't know how to call for help. We got us a bad situation here, Clint, and to tell you the truth, I'm worried more than a little bit. I want you to get on the radio and get Dustin, Jason, Jeremy, Luke and Brandon in here and make some kind of a plan to check these interstates and back roads all the way to the state line. If you run across anything and have to cross the line, let me know and I'll clear it for you. Now get started and keep me informed. The FBI will be in here this afternoon to get things rolling on a national scale, and we need to be ready for them. Let's go, and Clint, I'm depending on you".

Deputy Clint took one look at his boss and headed for the outer office. "Derek, get them boys in here pronto, we got us a mess". Derek nodded, and reached for the mike, "Boys, this is Derek.

Drop whatever it is you're doing and get back here. Harley wants us to start the ball rolling from this end on this Angela Leslie thing, and we need to have some kind of a plan. Smoke the tires boys this is serious stuff this time, and Jason, don't hit anything on the way in".

The rest of the deputies arrived and the plan was made to start cruising all the roads in the county and then switch to the interstate. Sheriff Wilson called the state police and filled them in on what everyone needed to look for. About two o'clock in the afternoon the FBI arrived and took over the investigation. The search was intensified locally with volunteers searching the fields and streams for Angela. Her picture was given to the local newspaper, who in turn called Indianapolis, and by evening the story was in the paper.

Harley decided it was time to pay another visit to Grandmother and Grandfather Leslie. He thought all the way out there about what he was going to say exactly but couldn't come up with anything that even sounded halfway good. "Might as well tell it like it is I reckon. We're looking at the worst and if it turns out to be nothing, well, that will be good news".

The dust rolled from behind his car driving up the long drive. It ran through his mind that he needed to wash his car every time he got on these back roads around Darlington. He had to smile though, this was such beautiful country around here he really didn't mind. Pulling into the yard brought grandmother and grandfather out onto the porch. Harley could tell Margaret was upset by the way she was curling her apron. "Evenin' folks. I came out to fill you in on the news".

Eight

They met up with Woody Miller just inside the New York state line, and the tractors were switched so it would be Ben's tractor that would be pulling Abraham's load west. When Woody was gone the three of them climbed into Abraham's tractor and started out for New York City itself. Angela was excited and seemed completely unaware of the problems she now faced. Both Benjamin and Abraham were going to try very hard to help her find her aunt, but if that failed they would have no other choice but to try and get her somewhere she would be safe. If that meant turning her over to the authorities, well then that is what they would have to do.

"How much further do we have to go, Ben"? She asked. "I can't wait to get to Aunt Mazie's house. She is a very good cook you know. We were there once on Thanksgiving, and she had the most wonderful tasting minced-meat pie. As soon as we get across the bridge I will ask someone where she lives".

Ben thought now was as good as time as any to explain to her that it would not be quite that simple. He decided to make an attempt to explain the situation so she would be able to understand exactly what they were in for. "Angela, if you had a toothpick that you had carried for a while and then put it back in the box with a thousand other toothpicks, do you think you could find that very one that you had in the beginning"? He looked over at Abraham and found him looking grim.

"Tooth picks. What was that? Have you lost your mind? Of course you couldn't find the same one. What kind of question was that to ask her anyway? We don't even have any toothpicks. Besides all toothpicks look alike. You and I couldn't even do that. Don't pay any attention to him Angela. He's losing his mind. I should have seen it coming before now. Lord, what am I doing here anyway"? Benjamin threw up his hands in frustration. "Can't you see I'm trying to explain something here Abe? We got us a situation here and I'm trying to explain it so Angela will understand what we are up against".

"My grandmother keeps toothpicks on the kitchen table in an old salt shaker. Grandfather uses them all the time," she said.

Ben applied the brakes so hard that had he not reached over and held Angela back she would have surely been thrown into the dash of the truck. Pulling to the side of the road, he set the brake and turned to face the little girl. His voice was stern and a little rough. "Angela, what did you just say"?

She was halfway through the sentence when she realized she had just given herself away. Thinking fast she tried to cover it up. "I meant the grandmother I used to have would do that. I haven't had anyone for a very long time now, Benjamin. Why are we stopping anyway? I would like to get to Aunt Mazie's today if you don't mind. Can we please get started again"?

Ben wasn't buying her story at all. "No I am not moving the tractor one foot until you tell me the truth, Angela. And I mean it, now talk".

Angela swelled up with anger and started screaming at him. "You can't talk to me that way! Who do you think you are! I don't need you, or Abraham either! Let me out this minute. I'll find someone else to help me. I hate you! I hate you too, Abraham! Let me out"! She started climbing over poor Abraham and was searching for the door handle. When she couldn't find it she started beating on the window of the truck. "Let me out! Let me out"!

Poor Abraham had never witnessed this behavior from her before and was scared half to death. His eyes grew very large, and opening the door, he leaped out himself. "You're both nuts you know that? Good Lord, what have I gotten myself into? Here I am stuck with two crazies and no place to go. You've got to get this thing straightened out Benjamin, or I ain't getting back into that truck". He was having trouble being heard because Angela was still screaming at Benjamin.

A trucker passing by noticed the tractor pulled off the side of the road and like most truckers do, he pulled his rig over and started to walk back to see if he could help in any way. Abraham saw him walk around the back of his trailer and not wanting to bring attention to themselves, hurried over to meet him. "Hey mister, what's up"? Abraham asked as he continued toward the well-meaning trucker.

The man shook hands with Abraham. "Howdy yourself. You got trouble with your truck there have you"? He started toward the tractor, but Abraham reached out and took hold of the man's arm stopping him. He was just about to speak when they both heard Angela scream. The man turned to look at the truck and then back toward Abraham. "Hey, what's going on here? Who do you have in that truck"?

Abraham knew he would have to do both some fast thinking and talking if they were even going to get to New York City, let alone stay out of jail. "Oh that. Ain't nothing mister. My partner there is just straightening out his daughter. We have been on the road quite a while, and she has been a rather big handful lately. Wanted to come on this trip, but all this time on the road has made her a bit cranky. Actually we're headed in to the city to drop her off at her Aunt Mazie's. She is going to stay there and go to school this next year. Very nice young lady but has a terrible temper". Abraham finished his hastily made up tale and smiled his biggest smile at the man.

All during his quickly made up story the man stood looking first at Abraham then at the truck from which the scream had come. "Uh huh," the man said, and turned toward the tractor where Benjamin was trying desperately to get control of Angela's temper. "I guess I'll just go and have me a look. And mister, if you are lying to me about this, I'm telling you right now, I'll get on the radio and call the state police. For all I know you might be kidnapping that child". The smile left Abraham's face and he had terrible visions of being locked in prison for the rest of his life. The man had started toward the waiting truck and all Abraham could do was spread his hands in a gesture of desperation and hope Ben would see him in time to get Angela under control.

Ben had been shifting his attention between Angela and Abraham when he saw the other trucker turn and start toward them. In a very stern voice he said, "Angela listen to me now, or this trip will be all over. There is a stranger coming toward the truck. If he believes you are in danger, he will call the police, and this trip will be over. Abraham and I will be put in jail, and you will be taken to a children's home and that will be it. If that is the way you want this trip to end, well, okay. If not, you better do some pretty quick thinking, and right now". He had just finished when the man opened the passenger door to the truck, looking first at Benjamin and then at Angela.

"What in the world is going on here? Mister, what are you doing with this child? I'm about two seconds from calling the state police. So this better be good".

Ben sat looking at the man not knowing what to say. He knew that any explanation from him right now would be useless. Sighing, he leaned back in his seat and waited. He too had visions of spending the rest of his life in jail.

Angela, hearing the tone of the man's voice, turned in his direction. "Just who are you, mister? And what business is it of yours what I am doing with my dad and Uncle Abraham anyway? For your information, they are taking me to my Aunt Mazie's house for a while. She lives in New York City just on the other side of the bridge that crosses over the river. Not that it is any of your business". When she had finished scolding the man, she leaned back against the seat and folded her arms across her chest.

The man stood looking at Angela with his mouth open in surprise. Turning to Benjamin she said, "Daddy, is the man still there"? Still leaning back against the seat Benjamin nodded his head and realized he had to speak. "Yes honey, he is still there". Again she turned toward the man. "Mister, can't you see that I am blind? My dad and I were having a conversation if you must know. It just so happens that sometimes I get mad at being blind and shout a little. My dad was just trying to calm me down is all, not that it is any of your business".

The man finally closed his mouth and spoke. "Sorry miss, it's just that your dad is...".

She cut him off. "My dad is what? Why don't you just go away and mind your own business". She then dismissed him altogether. "Uncle Abraham, are you out there with this retched man"?

Abraham seeing his chance spoke up quickly. "Why yes, child. Uncle Abraham is right here. Everything is going to be alright". Again he gave the stranger his biggest smile.

The other trucker shook his head in wonderment and turned to Abraham. Shaking his hand he apologized. "Sorry friend, I was just trying to help. Never know what you are going to run into out here. I have seen some strange things over the years. I'll just be on my way". He started to step away and then turned back. "Young lady, I can see from your attitude that you are indeed a handful. From the size of your dad there, my advice to you is to straighten up and mind what he says". The man nodded to Benjamin and started for his own rig.

Abraham leaped into the truck and sat down next to Angela. "Okay, that is going to do it for me. You two are plumb crazy. If either of you think for one minute that I am going to spend the rest of my life in jail for kidnapping, you have another think coming. Do you realize that if that man there called the police that our lives as we now know them would be over? Benjamin, I have seen you do some strange things in my time, but never anything like this. You have got to be clear out of your head and Angela, do you have any idea what the law would do to me and Ben if they caught us with you. We don't even know who your parents are. This has got to stop, and right now. Or I'm out of here".

Both men looked at her and saw the tears starting down her cheeks. She began to sob and not wanting to seem like a baby buried her face in her hands. Abraham threw his hands up in desperation and leaned back into his seat. "Okay, Ben, do something".

Angela spoke through her tears. "I don't have any parents if you want to know. They were killed when I was a baby. I was born blind, and I have been living with my grandmother and grandfather for as long as I can remember. They are getting old, and I decided to come and stay with Aunt Mazie for a while so they wouldn't have to work so hard. I knew that if I told you in the beginning, Benjamin, you wouldn't help me. We have come so far already. By this evening, I will be with Aunt Mazie, and you will be rid of me. Please take me the rest of the way".

Ben had been sitting quietly listening to her explanation. "Wait a minute, sis. Are you telling me that you have folks to look after you after all? When I picked you up back there in Indiana, you was running away from home"?

"Well yes, in a way I guess I was, but Benjamin, it isn't like it seems. I do have an Aunt Mazie and she does live across the bridge in New York City. She always wants me to come and spend some time with her, and we are almost there. You said so yourself. Please help me, Benjamin. I promise to call my grandparents as soon as I get to her house".

"Uh huh. And what is this bridge you keep talking about? There are at least three bridges in New York that I know of. Which bridge is it you mean exactly"?

"Oh that is easy, it is the bridge that goes across the Hudson River. Everyone there knows them, Ben. It will be easy to find where she lives. Will you please help me"?

Ben looked over at Abraham, who once again spread his hands in a gesture of frustration. "You do that a lot, you know that Abe? What's the matter with you anyway? Don't you want to help this child get to her aunt's? Get with the program".

Abraham looked surprised. "Oh yeah, well drive on James. We'll see how long we can stay out of jail".

Ben smiled at his longtime friend. "Look Abe, all we have to do when we get there is get the phone book and look up Aunt Mazie. We drop off Angela and head back out of town to pick up my truck. We might even have enough time to lay over a couple of days and take in some of the sights".

Angela reached over patted Benjamin on the arm, then turned and gave Abraham a hug. "Thank you both. I knew you would help me".

"Okay Angela, but you have got to stop that screaming stuff, you do. It scares me when you get to doing that. I ain't used to that kind of stuff. I like it nice and quiet. Isn't that right, Ben"?

"Yeah right," Ben said. "Angela, he plays the radio so loud when he's driving that he couldn't hear a police siren if it were driving alongside the truck".

Angela laughed. "Does it help you stay awake Abraham? All of that loud noise"?

This time Benjamin laughed. "Angela it not only keeps him awake, it keeps all the animals and everything else within a mile of him awake".

Abraham smiled good-naturedly. "It does keep me awake now that I think about it".

Nine

The big tractor wound its way along Interstate 95, then in the late afternoon New York City finally loomed on the horizon. Lights could be seen even from this distance. There is no other skyline in the world like that of New York. To a varying degree, it has inspired more than one entertainer to apply their talent trying to explain the effect it has had on their particular life.

Angela had fallen asleep leaning on Abraham. Ben reached over, and gently shaking her said, "There she is, Angela. New York City straight ahead". She sat straight up instantly awake and looked around. Ben thought to himself. "How difficult it must be for this little girl not to be able to see. Such excitement and energy. No wonder she has a temper. What good did all of this do if she can't see it"? It was then he remembered something he had learned a very long time ago from an old man who had been through a great deal himself. "Benjamin, everyone is made differently. No one sees or feels the same about anything. What is hard for one is easy for another. What is important for one is of no importance at all to another. As you go through life, Benjamin, you will do well to remember that. It will save you a whole lot of pain. Always remember that each of us has difficult times and things to face. Remember most of all, that we all are important".

"Is it as beautiful as Aunt Mazie said it was, Benjamin? Can you see the Statue of Liberty and the Empire State Building? What does it look like? Is the bridge still there? Stop and I will ask the first person we see where Aunt Mazie lives. Oh, we are close. I can just feel it".

Ben looked over at Abe and raised his eyebrows in frustration. "Sis, the thing you need to understand here is that New York may have grown some since your Aunt Mazie and her doctor husband moved here all those years ago. You see New York City alone has several million people living and working there. To just stop and ask anyone walking along on the street where they live, well, it most likely won't work. They would have no way of knowing where she might live. You see that don't you"?

Angela smiled and patted Ben's arm. "Oh, silly. It doesn't matter how many people have moved here in the past few years. Aunt Mazie hasn't moved and there is sure to be someone who knows her. Everyone knows their neighbors. Well, maybe not real well, but they are sure to know where someone lives on the block. Just drive across the bridge and stop the truck. I will ask around and we can be on our way".

It was evident that Angela had set her course and nothing Ben or Abraham said was going to make any difference. She had no way of knowing what several million people, meant, exactly. As far as she was concerned it was just an increase in the number of people that had moved into Aunt Mazie's neighborhood since the last time she had visited her. There was a real problem here and it seemed at least for now, there was no answer.

Abraham had an idea and decided to try and make Angela understand what they were up against here. "Angela, have you ever carried a bucket or a basket? Maybe one that you filled with sand or small stones or even dirt"?

"Why yes I have," she said. "I have used a basket, and a bucket, too. Why do you want to know that, Abraham"?

Abraham began to choose his words carefully. "Well, suppose you had found a certain very small stone by the creek where there were a great many other stones. If you put that stone in a bucket or basket and filled the basket or bucket up with all the other stones, think how hard it would be to find that very one that you had found before. That's what we mean when we say your Aunt Mazie is going to be hard to find".

Angela sat looking in his direction without expression. "I don't collect stones, Abraham. I don't believe Aunt Mazie collects them either. Though I do remember she has a few in her flower garden. Do you like to collect stones"?

Ben looked over at his friend and smiled. "Abe, you ain't the sharpest tack in the box. You know that? By the way, do you collect stones? We need to figure something out here about how to find Aunt Mazie. Get the map out and find the road we take to the bridge that goes to the island. Once we get there, we can look in the phone book and find the address. Can't be too hard if the guy was a doctor. Got to be some kind of address under his name".

Abraham nodded his agreement. "New York City is a big place, Ben. Those folks could be anywhere".

"Oh no," Angela said. "My Aunt Mazie lives in the Bronx. That's the reason everyone knows her. Everyone knows everyone that lives there. She will be very easy to find. You'll see".

"Okay, sis, the Bronx it is then. Abraham, we got to set our course for the George Washington Bridge. This is getting easier all the time. Angela, I reckon we'll be there before long".

Ten

Woody Miller was rolling west on Interstate 80, happy to be working, and happy to be driving Ben's big rig. Heaven Bound was a sweet truck. She was decked out with all the extras including an oversized sleeper with a television and even a sink with hot water. The local radio station was playing one of his favorite western songs, and he had it turned up loud enough that he couldn't hear the siren on the state police car that had been trying to get him pulled over for the last quarter of a mile. When he saw the state trooper in his side mirror, he slowed and pulled the big rig to the side of the road. Woody watched as the trooper walked up to the side of the tractor and looking up at him took off his sunglasses. "Driver, where you headed"?

"San Francisco, I reckon. Got a load to deliver before Saturday. Have I broken the law in some way, officer? I don't think I was speeding, and I haven't noticed anything wrong with the truck".

"No, you weren't speeding, driver. We are on the lookout for a truck that fits this description is all. Supposed to be out of Indiana somewhere. Seems that the driver is a big fellow, and has a small girl riding with him. Suspected kidnapping. Or a runaway I reckon. We're trying to find them before things get too far out of hand. Hand me down your log sheet will you"? Woody handed down the log sheet and when the state trooper saw that the tractor had logged time in Indianapolis, he stepped back and placed his hand on his pistol. "Driver, step down out of there. I am going to have a look inside the cab of your truck". Woody raised his hands and stepped down facing the trooper.

"I don't want no trouble, mister. All I'm doing is taking this load to San Francisco for a friend. If there is a problem I don't know nothing about it. Honest".

"Uh huh, suppose you just turn around there and let me put these handcuffs on until we get this straightened out. If there is no problem, you will be on your way in a few minutes". Woody turned

around and the trooper put the cuffs on. "Who is this friend
you're driving for anyway? What's his name"?
"Well sir, the man who is having me drive this rig here to
California is Abraham Morris".
The state trooper raised his eyebrows. "Is that so? I guess the
next question I have then is why is this truck registered to a
Benjamin Mansfield from Louisiana? This log says Abraham Morris
and the registration from the truck says Benjamin Mansfield.
Looks to me like you got some explaining to do here mister. You
want to start now? Or should we go back to the station"?
Woody knew that he was very close to being in serious trouble
with this policeman. He was going to have to do some very fast
and very truthful talking if he was to stay out of jail. Which would
not only be expensive and inconvenient for him, but for his friend
Abraham as well. Leaning over a little toward the trooper he
looked at the young man's badge to be sure of his name. "You see
Trooper Higgins, it's like this. This is not unusual as I am sure you
are aware of. This tractor here belongs to a Mister Benjamin
Mansfield. Mr. Mansfield has allowed Mr. Morris to use his
tractor to pull this trailer here to San Francisco, California. Mr.
Morris has hired me as his driver. As you can also see, my
licenses are all in order, and I believe you will find that my driving
record is without blemish. With that said, Woody smiled his best
smile at the trooper and waited for his answer.
Trooper Higgins looked at Woody's license and handed it back to
him. "You do have a point at that. Okay friend, I'm going to take
these cuffs off of you and let you go. Didn't mean to be so rough,
but we have a little girl missing, and I am just trying to do my job
here". Trooper Higgins unlocked the handcuffs and removed them.
Woody knew that his two friends were traveling with a small girl,
but he also knew they would never in their lives bother a child.
Both men were Christians, and they would try to help anyone in
trouble if at all possible. He knew that the trucker code was
important to them. Again he smiled his best smile and climbed

back up into the tractor. Without another word, he put the big rig into gear and pulled away. He didn't know exactly where his friends Abraham and Ben were, but he did know they were very close to being in very big trouble. Putting the big rig on cruise control at sixty-five miles an hour, Woody settled back and with the hood ornament pointed into the sunset, flipped his night lights on and concentrated on his Frisco run.

Eleven

Grandfather and Grandmother Leslie sat quietly in the living room thinking about their Angela. This was the third night without her, and they were very worried. They had never been without her even one night since she was given to them by the court after the tragic death of her parents so long ago. She was just one month old then and had never known any other parents but them. Grandmother Leslie looked up from her knitting to find grandfather staring at the evening paper. "Herbert, you have been on that same page from the time you sat down in that chair". Grandfather Leslie folded the paper and turned to look back at her. He could see the dark circles under her eyes put there by the lack of sleep. He knew her exhaustion was caused from worry, as was his. The thing he didn't know was what to do about it. Getting up from his chair he walked over and sat down beside her on the couch. Grandfather gently took her hands in his and pressed them to his heart. "Margaret, we have been together a very long time, and I want you to know that I love you very much. In all these years you are just as beautiful to me now as you were back when we were just youngsters trying to find our way. I know you hurt for Angela. So do I, but there is nothing we can do now but wait and see if she is found. We must be strong for her".

Turning her face toward him, grandfather wiped the tears from her eyes. She nodded in agreement. Grandmother was hurting very badly for Angela and through tears she whispered back to him, "I love you too, Herbert, but it has been three days since she has disappeared. Oh I pray she is all right. I think we should pray together for her safe return to us. Can we pray together Herbert"?

Grandfather Leslie nodded and together the two of them bowed their heads and asked the Heavenly Father to take care of their precious Angela. There, in the darkness of the countryside in a small farmhouse sat two old people praying for something they had no control over. They only knew they needed help from the Heavenly Father, so together they asked humbly for his help. When they were through, they thanked God for hearing their prayers and still holding hands, went in and prepared for bed. God would give them rest this night and perhaps tomorrow would bring news of Angela's safety. At least that was grandmother's thought as she drifted off to sleep. Grandfather Leslie lay quietly awake until he heard the slow even breathing of grandmother. Quietly raising himself up on one elbow, he gently brushed the few strands of white hair from her brow and kissed her forehead. "Goodnight, my love," he whispered as he lay back down and closed his eyes. In the darkness he couldn't see the smile that had come across her face. Her choice to have this gentle man all those many years ago had been a good one. Taking his hand in hers, she too, closed her eyes in sleep.

The morning brought the sun and clear skies. Grandmother Leslie, like all farm wives, was used to getting up early. Farmers start very early most of the time, and it was her job to see that Grandfather Leslie had a good breakfast to start his day. As she prepared it this morning her mind was on Angela once more, but this morning she had a good feeling about the day. Grandfather Leslie had finished shaving and as usual had managed to nick himself with his straight razor. When he came into the kitchen with toilet paper stuck to his neck, Grandmother Leslie laughed at him. "Herbert, you have been using that straight razor for almost fifty years, and I don't believe I have ever seen you shave without nicking yourself somewhere. Do you think you will ever get it right"?

He felt the paper on his neck and laughed himself. "Well, if I keep trying I think I'll get the hang of it one of these days. My father used this same razor all his life, and it did well for him. I see no need to change the way I do things now".

"Is that right? Well, the only thing I can say is don't sneeze while you're shaving. I really don't want the mess on the bathroom floor". She set their plates on the table and pulled out a chair. Grandfather looked at her and could see she was feeling better this morning. "My, ain't we spry this morning. Feel better do you"?

She squeezed his hand and smiled. "You know, I really do. It must have been the little talk we had last night with God. Also it could have been the kiss you gave me last night. I could use a little more of that".

"Is that so? Well, we'll just have to see about that. Right now though I have to get the milking done. I need to go into town today after some fence wire. Thought you might like to go for a change". Grandfather finished his breakfast and put on his boots and milking jacket and started out the door. He paused and turned back around. "I could be wrong, but I have a good feeling about this thing this morning, Margaret. I'll be done in a couple of hours. Be ready to go".

She walked over and kissed him on the cheek. "Don't you worry about me, Herbert. I've been ready for you all my life". Smiling, he nodded and walked out the door toward the barn.

Twelve

The big truck entered the city in darkness. Ben never tired of looking at the skyline of New York City. Most especially at night. The lights of the big buildings seemed to wink and twinkle as he drove along. At street level there were all manner of colored lights advertising the wares and services of those in business. Abraham too, was impressed with the number of people still walking about and doing business, even at this late hour. "She never seems to sleep, Ben. I don't think I have ever been here when there weren't people out and about. Big and beautiful. No other way to describe it".

It was late as the big tractor moved slowly down the avenue. As they moved closer to the boroughs, traffic began to thin out some and there were less and less people on the streets. As in all cities there were areas that were in need of repair and renovation. These areas, full of shadows, danger and crimes of all sorts, are a haven for those who prey on others. Only the foolish venture into these alleyways of crime and expect to emerge safely. As the big truck moved slowly along, shadowy figures quickly stepped out of the headlights that seemed to cut its way through the darkness. Ben drove through this area and into a more desirable part of town. It was now very late, and Angela had long since crawled into the big truck's bunk behind them, and was now very much asleep. Pulling the truck into the deserted parking lot of a large grocery store, Ben turned the engine off and both men leaned back to get some much-needed rest. Just before he drifted off to sleep, Abraham said softly, "Partner, it feels good helping this child. No money in it, but it sure feels good".

Ben smiled and nodded his agreement. "Uh huh, this is the kind of stuff that goes in the good book buddy. Things like this don't come along very often. Most times when someone needs help folks just seem to turn away. That's the reason for so many homeless folks. Nobody wants to get involved and those who do are spread awfully thin". Benjamin drifted off to sleep thinking of their childhood growing up walking dirt roads and fishing the beautiful ponds and rivers of the Deep South. That was so very long ago. Angela woke up hungry shortly after three in the morning. She leaned close to first one then the other of the men. Their slow even breathing told her they were fast asleep. Lying back down she tried her best to be still, but the excitement of being close to her Aunt Mazie's and not being there, was almost more than she could bear. Slipping her coat on, she very carefully crawled out of the bunk and eased her way around Abraham. Being blind, moving around things without destroying them had been learned many years ago. It seems to be something that develops in blind people. Moving things or putting things back becomes second nature to them just as it does to those with sight.

*I remember my first encounter with a blind person. As a youngster, the town I lived in, Chula Vista, California, had open-air storefronts. Each day the store owners would roll up or pull up their storefronts getting ready for the business of the day. Back then Chula Vista was a rather small town and most all of the businesses were on the main street that ran through town. On Saturday morning after my chores were done, I would leave from my house on Carla Avenue and follow Hilltop Drive to Main Street. At the Catholic school I would make a left turn and in a short while I would be downtown. The stores would all be open and as you walked along you could see from the fronts of the stores clear to the back. I liked that very much. On one of the corners there was a newspaper stand that was owned by a blind man. I remember standing and watching this man sell his papers and magazines to passersby. As I watched, he would somehow make change from dollar bills, five-dollar bills and others. I was always amazed at how he could tell the difference. After several times of watching him I finally asked how he was able to do that, as he couldn't see. Smiling, he told me it was a secret. I walked on up the street to the Vogue Theater and my usual Saturday matinee, but from that time on I always stopped to watch this man work what appeared to be magic, with his cash register.

Quietly opening the door she slipped out. Standing on the step, she carefully pressed it the door closed and lowered herself to the pavement. Listening to the sounds around her she was able to tell about where the street was and knowing that in a city this size where there was a street there was bound to be a sidewalk. Slowly she started toward the sounds of the traffic intending to ask the first person she met where her Aunt Mazie lived.

In this city, as in all large cities, there are those who live off of the misery and pain of others. One must be very careful in such places. As it happened just now, there was, walking along this mostly deserted and quiet part of town, just such a person. As one might imagine, this person was a product of the dark and shadowy night he worked in. Dressed in dark clothing this person was almost invisible to the innocent passerby. His black stocking cap completed his outfit, and unless you knew him by name he would be, by his design, impossible to recognize. A mean and sinister man indeed. And right now he was moving in on his prey like a cat would sneak up on an unsuspecting mouse.

A smile came across his face as he stood and watched this little girl slip out of the big truck and lower herself to the ground. Instantly a plan formed in his mind. "This would indeed be a very profitable night," he whispered to himself, as he began to quicken his pace closing the distance between himself and Angela.

Hearing someone behind her, Angela stopped and turned around waiting on whoever it was. This would be her chance to find out where her Aunt Mazie lived. "Hello there," she said, smiling, as the man came ever closer. "I'm glad you came along just now. Would you mind helping me? I am looking for someone who lives near here".

The man stood looking at her in surprised disbelief. "This child is blind for pete's sake. She has no idea where she is or even who or what I am," he thought to himself as he stood in front of her.

"Hello yourself, little girl. How may I help you? Am I mistaken, or are you blind"?

"No Sir, you are not mistaken. I have been blind from birth, but it doesn't bother me much most of the time. I have been traveling for some time, and now that I am finally here in New York. I need to ask where my Aunt Mazie lives. Do you know her"?

The chilly excitement of anticipation washed over him. "Could this be real? This can't possibly be happening in this city. No one is this dumb as to ask strangers about someone. Especially if they are blind as is this one," he thought. Speaking as calmly as he could, he answered her. "Well, young lady, I know a lot of people who live around here, but I surely don't think I know anyone by the name of Aunt Mazie. Does this Aunt Mazie have a last name? If she does it would sure be a big help".

"Why yes," said Angela smiling up at him, "her name is Mrs. Mazie Carter. She is married to a Doctor Richard Carter. Does that help you"?

Faking excitement he clapped his hands together and exclaimed. "Mazie Carter! My goodness why didn't you say so in the beginning. Why everyone around here knows of Dr. and Mrs. Carter. They live not fifteen minutes from here. Would you like me to take you there now"?

Angela thought for a second before she responded. "Well, I do want to see them. But Benjamin and Abraham would worry if I were to leave and not tell them where I was going. Besides I want them to meet Aunt Mazie. I'll just go wake them and we can all go".

She started back to the truck, but the man took hold of her arm and turned her back around. "Wait," he said, "I have a better idea. It looks to me as if you folks have driven a long way and your two friends are tired from the trip. Suppose you and I go and see your Aunt Mazie and then we can come back and get them. That way they can get their rest before meeting her. I will leave them a note telling them where we are so they won't worry. How does that sound to you"?

"Well, that will be alright I suppose. Benjamin and Abraham have been very busy with me. Yes, that is a good idea".

Again this evil man clapped his hands together in mock excitement. "Good girl. You just wait here and I will leave a small note telling them where we are going. Now don't move, there is a lot of traffic here, and I don't want you to get hurt. Just stand real still until I return". The man was gone for just a short time, then returned and took Angela's hand. Together they started down the dark street away from where Benjamin and Abraham were sleeping, fading into the shadowy dangers of the big city.

Thirteen

Woody Miller had reached his destination in California. He unhooked the trailer in the delivery yard of the company that had been waiting its delivery, got his paperwork signed and he was ready to start back to meet Abraham and Ben to switch back the truck tractors. Woody was tired and knew he needed sleep, but he also knew his friends were unaware they were being hunted for kidnapping. He also knew he had to reach them before it was too late. The best thing to do was get a couple of hours sleep and then start out from there. Two or three hours sleep would put him on the interstate around midnight. He reckoned he would be able to make better time then. Besides he needed sleep. To wreck the tractor due to lack of sleep wouldn't help anyone, so he pulled the bunk curtain and, after setting the alarm for midnight, crawled into the bunk.

At midnight the alarm woke him. After splashing some water on his face, he started the truck and pulled out onto the street that led to the eastbound interstate. It took about forty minutes for him to clear local traffic and blend in with the rest of the big rigs headed east. Pulling into the first truck stop, he purchased a couple of sandwiches and a bag of chips. He had his thermos filled with hot coffee and, after washing up a bit, climbed back into his rig and started out again.

Needing to make good time he got on the radio and asked for a break. "Break westbound for Heaven Bound". Well, everyone knew who Heaven Bound was and his radio cracked back.

"That you big Ben? You're out of your area ain't you? Thought you were running the Midwest these days".

Woody came back. "This ain't Ben, friend. I'm a friend of his and I need to make some time. How's your back door"? [In trucker's talk, this means are there any policemen sitting anywhere close to where you have just come through.]

His radio cracked back. "Back door is fine friend". [When truckers refer to the back door they are talking about the road they have just traveled over.] "Chicken coops [chicken coops are the weigh stations that are placed every so often on roads to enable law enforcement officers to make sure the trucks are not overloaded] are closed until morning, I guess. Roll on".

Woody said he was obliged, and made his decision. Pushing down on the pedal, he wound the big truck up to around eighty miles an hour. At this speed the big diesel was singing a sweet song to him. He smiled and listened as Heaven Bound hummed along. Slowing down only for congested areas or when old Smoky was around, he drank coffee and carefully worked his way east. At this rate if he didn't get stopped, he would be able to meet Ben and Abraham some time the following day, or at the latest, the day after.

Around four in the morning he decided to see if he could get a relay message to Ben or Abraham. Again he grabbed the mike.

"Breaker nineteen for Heaven Bound".

Once again the radio cracked back. "Go ahead break. I gotcha Heaven Bound".

Woody thanked the driver and asked if this message could be relayed east to Desert Runner, which was Abraham's CB handle. "From Heaven Bound I'm eastbound and down. Remember Lincoln on Halloween".

The trucker said he would start the relay, and Woody listened as he put out the message. It would take a while, but Woody knew Abraham would get the message. Smiling he remembered the time old man Lincoln had called the law on them both of them for getting into his melon patch just before Halloween night, years ago. It wasn't serious, but they shouldn't have done it and both knew the local law was looking for them.

Fourteen

Sheriff Wilson had not had much sleep in the past three nights. He had either been in his car or in the office talking to other enforcement agencies that were helping. This was a small town and frankly he had not had this kind of thing happen before. Oh, there had been a car theft now and again or a filling station would be robbed by some passerby on occasion, but nothing this serious had ever happened here. Thinking back he could remember when old man Thomas had accidentally shot himself while climbing a fence during hunting season, but that was about it. So it was a real job dealing with the townspeople during this ordeal.

Call after call had come in from frightened housewives fearing little Johnny or Sally had been taken if they were five minutes late. It was a pain, but he did understand the problem. His deputies were also doing their best to keep things under control. All and all, this was turning into a mess. The mayor had reminded him he would be coming up for election in a couple of months and if this wasn't cleared up by then, one way or the other, it wouldn't look good. Thinking on it for a moment he decided he didn't care how it looked for the mayor. As a matter of fact, the mayor could go jump in the lake for all he cared. The girl was the one with the problem now, and the mayor had darned well better realize it. Grabbing a cup of coffee, he headed out the door to his car and started out of town to see Margaret and Herbert again. The one thing he wanted to do was keep them informed. Driving up the lane he saw Margaret open the screen door. By the time he got out of his car she was sitting on the porch swing. She nodded a small greeting as he walked up the three steps and sat down beside her. "No news, Margaret. Just thought I would come out myself and tell you. Didn't want to call on the phone. I don't like doing that. I'll tell you, I have never seen anything like this before. I feel lost here trying to deal with this thing. There doesn't seem to be any leads at all. Oh, a deputy stopped a trucker in Illinois yesterday, but he was of no help at all. Didn't even fit the description. Sorry about all of this ma'am".

Grandmother Leslie patted his arm and smiled. "James, I have known you all your life. Your mother and I went to school together in Darlington not so long ago. I happen to know you are a good man and are doing all you can about this terrible thing that has happened. I'm going to get you a cold glass of lemonade, and you and I will just sit here and rest for a while. To tell you the truth I could use the company". Grandmother Leslie left and returned with some molasses cookies and two glasses of lemonade. Sitting back down beside him she once again patted his arm and asked about his children.

It had been a pleasant break. Grandmother Leslie had a way of making big problems seem a bit smaller. Driving back to town he thought about all the times he had slept over at the farm while he was growing up. It had been his second home really. Good people. Very good people. He vowed to solve this mess one way or the other. "I owe them that," he whispered as he drove along.

Fifteen

As night passed, the dim and shadowy streets had gradually given way to dawn. The sky was pink with the morning sun when Abraham's eyes opened. Turning to check on Angela, he saw the bunk where she had been sleeping so soundly just a short time before was empty. He tapped Ben on the shoulder. "Hey partner, what have you done with Angela"?

Benjamin was instantly awake and looking around. "Her coat is gone. Did you let her out? I mean maybe she had to go to the bathroom or something. Lord, has that child run off"? It was then that he noticed the piece of paper that the stranger had slipped under the windshield wiper. He opened and read it, then sat looking out the windshield in stunned silence. "She's been kidnapped, Abe. That little girl has been kidnapped for crying out loud"!

Abraham reached for the note, read it and leaned back against the seat. "Well, if it's any consolation the kidnapper ain't much of a go getter, Ben. He only wants fifty dollars. In this neighborhood that makes somebody who just wants a supply of whiskey or wine for a couple of days. We have the money. Let's go get her back".

Ben was angry and it showed. His massive frame was rigid with anger. "Abe, being a bum makes this guy no less dangerous. One thing is for sure though, he ain't going to go too far if he lives in this neighborhood. On the other hand he could have killed her by now and just gone his way. This note says we are to leave the money in a can behind the dumpster at the corner of Eleventh Street and Montgomery Avenue. Wherever that is? Let's drive down the street a ways and see if we can locate the place".

The corner where the money was supposed to be left was easy enough to find, and the dumpster behind the building was there where it was supposed to be. Easy enough, except for one small thing. Both men seemed to notice it at the same time. Abraham

was the first to speak. "So, after we leave the money, when do we get Angela back? I mean does he just send her to us or what"?
Ben shook his head in disgust. "Abe, I have been thinking of calling the cops. I mean this child ain't even mine and here she is gone. We've been seen over half the country with this little girl and if they stop us and want to know where she is, well, what do you suppose they will think"?
Ben looked over at his friend and could see the little beads of sweat that had suddenly appeared on his forehead. "That's jail time, Ben, big time. We have got to get her back and right now. We had better put this truck somewhere out of sight and start out on foot looking for her". Ben nodded his agreement and put the tractor in gear.
Parking the truck beside the hulk of an old burned-out garage, they locked it up and made their plans. "Abe, I got us in this mess so I intend to do the leg work. What I would like for you to do is make yourself look like you belong around here, and park yourself in a spot where you can watch that dumpster. Put the money in the can and if the guy comes after it, you can follow him and bring back Angela. I'm going to start out and go building to building until we run out of time. Keep in prayer on this, buddy. We need all the help we can get. One more thing, no cops on this one. You run this guy down, you handle it. I'll do the same thing if I run across him". Abraham nodded, and they walked away from each other. It took Abe about ten minutes to find someplace to hide. Actually, he didn't hide at all. Reaching down he grabbed a handful of dirt. Rubbing some in his hair and the rest on his coat and pants, he sat down on the sidewalk in plain view. He leaned his back up against the wall of an abandoned building where he could see the dumpster and across the street from a hole-in-the-wall bottle store. If the guy stopped at the can for the money, he figured it was a sure bet his next stop would be the store. When that happened, there was no doubt in Abraham's mind, he would tell him where Angela was. In the meantime, he had nothing else to do but wait.

About noon, another resident of the area walked up and sat down beside him. He looked Abe over and laughed. "My friend, you need a bath. Being poor is no excuse for being dirty you know. I had an Aunt one time who always said, cleanliness is next to Godliness. Have you ever heard that saying friend"?

Abraham was in no mood for this and growled at the stranger. "Mister, clean or not, I don't like you. Now you get away from me or I'm going to clean up on you. Have you ever heard that saying friend"?

The stranger put his hand up and acted as if he had been slapped across the face. "Well, you're not a very hospitable fellow are you? I was merely waiting for Lord Ashcroft to come by this morning and pick up his usual bottle. He shares a small amount with me on a daily basis and I was going to suggest to him that you might like some as well. No matter now though. It is ilk like you that ruins the neighborhood. I shall remember your poor manners, friend".

Abraham didn't respond, but watched as the man walked all of ten feet away and sat down again, being sure he had a good view of the bottle store. Abraham thought to himself how unfortunate it is when we allow ourselves to be controlled by anything that is able to destroy us. His memory returned to childhood when he would watch as his father consumed alcohol to the point where he had no control over his speech or movements. How he used to wish his father would spend time with him and his sister, instead of the bottle. A sad time in their lives, turned even more so, when his father drowned one day while driving back from town after he had spent the day drinking with a friend. He had been driving much to fast for the road he was on and, losing control of his car, plunged down an embankment into the river below. The car was found several hundred yards down river, but his father was never found. He would wonder later if his father had escaped the tragedy and used the opportunity to just run off. The funeral service at the empty grave brought about a promise to himself never to put his own family through that horrible experience.

At about three in the afternoon, Abraham watched as a man dressed in dark clothing moved slowly up the opposite side of the street. When he came close to the dumpster, he hesitated and looked around. The hair on the back of Abraham's neck raised, and he began to slowly ready himself for a chase in case this was the man who had taken Angela and demanded the money. The second the man reached for the can, Abraham uncoiled like a spring and started sprinting across the thirty or so yards toward him.

The kidnapper grabbed the can, pocketed the money, and threw the can in the dumpster. Had he not been so weary, Abraham would have been able to grab him there and then, but this was not the case. Thieves, like animals, are always weary of being caught and this was the case with this man as well. He saw Abraham running toward him and like a frightened animal bolted away. A smile came to Abraham's lips when he saw the frightened man's stride. Putting on even more speed he was able to run the man down within thirty yards. Working his way up behind him he launched himself into the air and came down hard on the kidnapper's back sending them both to the ground. In an instant, Abraham had the man turned over and was sitting on his stomach looking into the man's eyes. "I'm just going to ask you this once, mister, and if I don't get the answer I want I am going to hurt you very badly. Where is the little girl you took from the truck"? The man continued to struggle, and as angry as Abraham was at that moment, he slapped the man very hard on the side of the head. "Listen you, that child is blind and you knew that when you took her. You think that little slap was something, if you don't tell me right now where she is, I'm going to hurt you bad. Where I come from they hang people like you and let them rot in the tree. NOW! Where is she"?

The man had had all he wanted of Abraham and his tactics. Just as Abraham drew his fist back to strike, the man decided to talk. "I took her to an old, abandoned apartment building up the street. She is tied up on the third floor. She's scared, but not hurt. At least not yet. There are a lot of people who use that place for drug sales and go in and out all the time. Don't know how long she will be safe".

Abraham was so angry he was shaking all over. "You filthy scum. I ought to beat you to death right here. You stole that child for wine". Jerking the man to his feet, he shoved him roughly ahead of him. "Get moving and I mean right now. Walk fast mister or you won't make it at all, and if there is anything at all wrong with that child you aren't going to make it anyway. I have a mind to just leave you for the rats the way it is. Now move"!

Benjamin had been walking the streets and back alleys since early morning talking to anyone who would listen. Sometime around three o'clock in the afternoon he stopped and questioned an old woman pushing a shopping cart full of what looked to be glass bottles and cans. After some conversation, she told him that she thought she had heard what sounded like a crying child coming from an old, abandoned apartment building she had passed. As it turned out, it was located on a corner that Ben had passed several times that day.

He thanked the woman and began to run toward the building praying that Angela was still there and unharmed. Reaching the front of the building he stopped and listened. Hearing nothing he stepped quietly through the front door and listened again. Still he heard nothing. Tears filled the big man's eyes and he shook his head in sorrow. He must find her! He must! "Angela," he called out. "Angela, are you here girl? Father, help me find her. Please help me find her". It was then he heard it. Ever so faintly. A soft whimper. Then another! It was her! He knew it! One, two, no, three flights up! Filled with energy, he bounded up those stairs like he was ten years old once again. At each floor he would listen again and call out. "Angela, I'm coming girl, talk to me"! Each time she would call out to him. "I'm here Benjamin, I'm here. Please hurry". And hurry he did. When he reached the third floor, he was surprised to see several people sitting on the floor of the hallway. They seemed to be doing all sorts of things, but he didn't stop to investigate, he just kept walking and calling out to her. At the far end of the hall he found a locked door, and listening he could hear her sobbing and calling his name as best she could.

With one huge hand he grabbed the doorknob and twisted. The power in his hand broke the knob and the lock and the door opened a little. Carefully he pushed it open. There, sitting on the floor, tied up with electrical cord, was little Angela. The kidnapper had put some kind of tape over her mouth but she had worked it loose to be able to call out. Looking at her he could see she was filthy but unharmed. Her arms were tied behind her back, and her ankles had been taped as well. Fighting to contain his rage at whoever had done this, he walked across the room and knelt down beside her. Very gently he began taking off her restraints. "It's me, Angela, I'm here". Tears had made clean marks down her otherwise dirty face.

"Oh, I knew you would come, Benjamin. I told that awful man you would come and get me. Where is Abraham? Did he come with you"? Benjamin finished untying her and very gently picked her up. So overcome was he by the sight of Angela that he couldn't speak. All he could do was hold her gently in his huge arms and let his own tears fall from his eyes. Angela felt him sob and placed her tiny hand on his cheek. Feeling his tears she said nothing and placed her arms around his neck, squeezing tightly. Together they left the room and walked back down the stairs and out into the afternoon sunlight.

Sixteen

Abraham and the kidnapper had just rounded the corner next to the building. The man took one look at the size of Benjamin and the girl he was holding and started to bolt away. Reaching out, Abraham grabbed him by the back of the neck and jerked him back. Roughly pushing the man up against the side of the building, he looked into the man's eyes. "You see that big man there, mister. He wants to talk to you. And, if I were you I would listen real good. You hear me, mister"? The man shook his head in agreement and stood trembling as Benjamin walked over to where Abraham stood holding the man. Benjamin handed Angela gently to Abraham, then reached out and taking hold of the front of the man's shirt, lifted him off the ground. So frightened was the man he wet himself. Benjamin looked down at the puddle of water forming beneath the man and then back into his face.

Knowing they were already most likely in a bad predicament, Benjamin knew he would have to handle this situation carefully. "Mister, what's your name anyway? I like to know who it is that I'm talking to. Especially when they have decided to hurt a friend of mine". The man still hanging in the air decided it was best not to lie to this giant. "Name's Nathan Whitehall. You going to hurt me, mister"? Benjamin smiled up at the man. "Mister Whitehall, my friends and I are very busy people so we don't have a lot of time here. You are from this neighborhood and so I am going to give you some very friendly advice. I drive my truck through here all the time making deliveries on this side of the river. My advice to you is to relocate to another part of town, or better yet, move clear out of the state. You see, you hurt my little friend here and the only reason I'm not snapping your neck like you deserve is because we don't have time to haul you off somewhere. Now on the other hand, if I come through here and see you again I will take the time and do just that. Is that clear, mister"?

The kidnapper was so frightened that he began to smell from something else that became more unpleasant with each passing second. But he also saw that he wasn't going to be hurt badly and began to vigorously shake his head in agreement. "Well, we are certainly grateful for your understanding of this situation mister. With that Benjamin released the hold he had on the man's shirt, and he fell in a heap at his feet. "Get moving, Mister Whitehall, and don't cross my path ever again". Wet from his own water and stinking from his own bowel movement, the man leaped to his feet and began running down the street. Abraham stood for a moment watching him and then the three of them started back to the truck to continue their search for Angela's aunt. "You know, Ben, that fellow sure did stink. Needs to change his diet a bit if you ask me".

Seventeen

Abraham's truck was like many trucks of today. In the sleeper part of the truck was a small sink with soap and towels. They pulled the curtains, and Angela spent the much-needed time cleaning the dirt off herself. Ben stopped the big truck across from a local laundromat, and Angela handed him her clothes so he could wash them. The sight of the two men washing a small girl's clothes did draw some stares, but that was all.

Back on the road once again, they headed for the area where Angela had told them her Aunt Mazie lived. Once there, they parked the big tractor and began trying to gather information as to just where her aunt might live. Checking the phone book brought no results at all, and the few people they asked had never even heard of a Doctor Carter or his wife. The rest of the afternoon was spent asking first one person then another until Benjamin and Abraham had just about given up. Thinking about it for a minute, Benjamin decided to tell Angela the truth. The problem was in the fact that they were almost two thousand miles from where he had picked her up, and he knew that unless they found her Aunt Mazie they would have to leave her with the police or child services, or someone who would take care of her. Considering the situation they were now in, he decided to try something else.

"Angela, didn't you say that your aunt's husband was a doctor here for a long time? He treated patients around here somewhere. Isn't that right"?

"Yes, he took care of this whole area for a very long time. Dr. Richard Carter. He isn't alive anymore though. My grandmother brought me to his funeral when I was very little. Aunt Mazie is the only one living here now".

"Well, if he lived and worked in this area, he would have had to write prescriptions for his patients. So, the thing I need to do is find a drugstore and ask where his office was. That will at least give us an address. Tell you what, Abe, you and Angela pick up some sandwiches and some cold drinks and I will try and find a drugstore. It's getting late and we need to eat. With any luck we can drive right to the house in the morning. How does that sound, Angela"?

"I am hungry, and tired too. It sounds just fine, Benjamin. Without you and Abraham's help I never would have found Aunt Mazie". Pulling the big man's hand over against her cheek, she looked up at him and smiled. "Thank you, Benjamin".

The big man looked over at his friend. "Take care of her Abe, I'll be back soon".

"Consider it done. Nothing else is going to go wrong. We've had enough excitement for one day. Go do what you have to do. The food will be here when you get back".

Abraham had spotted a sandwich shop earlier in the day and after putting Angela in the truck, he explained that she was not to open it for anyone. "Ben and I have the keys and we will unlock it when we need to get back in. You don't open this door for anyone. It's very important that you leave it locked, Angela. Do you understand"?

"Yes Abraham, I will leave it locked. That mean man might come back. But why can't I just come with you"?

Abe rubbed his chin and thought for a second. "Well, for one thing it is very dark out here, and we don't want to lose you again. For another, this is a bad part of town after dark and that makes me worry about you. So, I will lock the door and be back in a jiffy. Okay"?

"Yes, but please hurry back".

Locking both doors, Abraham headed for the sandwich shop on the next block. Returning a few minutes later, he found Angela asleep. Looking at the girl resting so peacefully, he let his mind wander back quite few years to when he was lad about this age. Nothing seemed to bother children the way it does adults. Carefully he wrapped her sandwich up and set it aside for her to eat later.

Smiling to himself he said, "You do have a good appetite, young lady".

Benjamin thought he might already know the answer to what he was trying to find out before he ever reached the pharmacy store. A few words with the druggist confirmed what he already knew. Angela's aunt and uncle were both dead. Her uncle had died several years before, and her aunt had passed away just last year. He did manage to find out where they were buried though, and he determined he would tell Angela about her aunt's death. He knew this would be a shock to the little girl, but she was now alone and there were some considerations that needed to be made. One very big one was looming ever closer, and try as he might, he knew it would have to be faced sooner or later. His life had always been trucking, trucking all over the country and Canada for that matter, and there was just no place for a small blind girl to fit in his life, regardless of how attached he had become to her. On the other hand, to leave this little one in the hands of strangers seemed almost mean. Especially strangers that she couldn't even see. A worried frown came over Ben's face and remained there all the way back to the truck.

Eighteen

Abraham spotted his friend when he was still a block away, and smiled to himself. "Man, he is big". Remembering all the times when he and Benjamin had walked together in the old neighborhood, Abraham couldn't remember a time when Ben had turned anyone down who needed help. Shaking his head he said aloud, "Big, gentle giant. Yep, Ben the giant".

When Benjamin reached the truck he stood outside long enough to worry Abraham. Opening the door, Abraham quietly lowered himself to the ground so as not to wake Angela. He could see the worried look on his friend's face and knew there must be a problem. "What's the matter pard? Couldn't find the address? We can always check another pharmacy. Got to be somebody who knew the Doc".

Benjamin leaned up against the truck and looked at his friend. "That ain't it Abe. I went to the right pharmacy all right. As a matter of fact, even the cashier remembered the doc and his wife. Good people too I guess. Least ways that's what they said. The thing is Aunt Mazie died almost a year ago. Even told me where they were buried. Now we got to tell this little blind girl that she has no one left in her life here. I don't like that, Abe. Not even a little. We got to think of something, and quick. This is going to hit her hard".

"Ain't nothin' to do but be honest with her, Ben. After that we will just have to do what's best for her, and you know that means child services. They have people to handle these kinds of things. Who knows? Maybe she will find a good home"?

"Well, there it is," thought Ben. "Once again old Mr. Reality rears his ugly head and hurts someone else. I have been dealing with this kind of thing, it seems all my life, and it never gets any easier. Someone special always gets hurt".

Reaching up, he opened the driver's side door and looked at Abe. "Let's get this over with. I got work to do, and it ain't waitin'".

Angela sat quietly and listened as Ben explained that it would not be possible for her to stay with her Aunt Mazie. When he told her that Aunt Mazie had died last year, tears flooded her eyes and ran down her cheeks. Ben hadn't been prepared for what happened next. Angela reached for the big man and putting her arms around his neck, simply said, "Benjamin, I want to go home. I want you and Abraham to take me home". And then she began to sob.

Ben looked at Abe, and the tears in his friend's eyes did nothing to clear the lump in his own throat. However, the seriousness of the moment, and the statement Angela had just made, did. He suddenly realized that here he and Abraham were, in the middle of New York City, in a very large truck with a twelve-year-old blind girl who was telling them that she wanted to go home. Suddenly, Benjamin was angry. Very angry. The seriousness of the situation they were in suddenly hit him. If Angela had a home and she was now with two grown men that could mean that folks would think they had kidnapped this little girl. One look at Abe told him that they were thinking the same thing. Both of them could quite possibly be spending a very long time in prison!

Abraham's voice was very calm, but firm. "Angela, where is home? Where do you live"?

"Rockville, Indiana. I live there on a farm with my Grandfather and Grandmother Leslie. It's the house right where you picked me up Benjamin".

Benjamin's face had been buried in his hands. "Oh Lord, sis, do you realize what you have done? Do you realize that Abraham and me could spend a very long time in prison for kidnapping you"?

Angela was puzzled about that. "What is kidnapping? Is that a bad thing"?

"Oh yes, sis, kidnapping is a very bad thing. It means taking someone against their will. Taking someone when they don't want to go".

Angela smiled. "Well then, you have nothing to worry about. I wanted to go. So, let's go home now. You and Abraham can take me home".

Benjamin made his decision quickly. "Abe, we are supposed to meet Woody at the rest park on the Lincoln Exchange route. We can switch tractors there and head Heaven Bound for Canada. It's a long shot, but if we make the border without being stopped we can skip across Canada and drop down into one of the states and head for Indiana. With any luck we can make it in twenty-four hours if we switch off driving".

Abraham shook his head in wonderment. "Ben, we've been friends it seems like forever, and there ain't much I wouldn't do for you, but if you get caught or even stopped in Heaven Bound for any reason at all, you are going to prison. I can't risk that old friend, not even for you. I just plain have too many people depending on me. I feel bad about it, but I must take care of business".

"I do understand old friend. When we meet up with Woody, we'll part company there and you have my thanks for all you've done".

"Nothin' more than you would have done for me. Been kind of exciting really. Enjoyed it. Well mostly".

The rest park on the Lincoln Exchange was dark and full of trucks set for the night by the time they arrived. The switch was made, and Ben climbed into the seat of Heaven Bound, fired up the big diesel. After seeing that Angela was tucked in the big sleeper, Ben put the huge tractor in gear and waved goodbye to his friend.

Nineteen

Ben smiled as the big tractor responded to his hands. He had been driving this truck for many years. She wasn't as shiny and new as others he had seen, but she was in perfect shape and had been his for several years now.

Heading north, Ben set the speed just above the speed limit so as not to attract attention. Most big rigs crowd the speed limit to cut as much time as possible off the driving time to their destination. The big tractor hummed along happily into the night, passing first one town then another. It was about three in the morning when they pulled into the checkpoint at the border between the U.S. and Canada. Angela had been awake for some time and was complaining about being hungry. Ben explained that they would stop for breakfast sometime after they crossed over into Canada. At the checkpoint, a customs officer walked up to the tractor and looked her over before coming to Ben's side of the truck. "What's your business here in Canada, mister? Picking up a load headed for the U.S., I imagine"?

Ben had been at this trucking business for a long time and knew what the next question would be and he was ready. "No sir, not this time. Normally I head on into Quebec and pick up a load of yard goods and return to New York. But this time I'm going on into the city to sell this old girl and perhaps pick up a newer tractor. Hate to do it though, we have been together for a long time".

"I see, well, she seems to be in good shape. I do like her name. Heaven Bound has a nice ring to it. You a Christian, mister"?
"For about as long as I can remember. Don't know what folks do that aren't".

The customs man reached up and shook hands with Ben and motioned him on through the checkpoint. He could see the man waving a goodbye as he pulled away. Ben shifted gears and waved back, then settled into the job at hand, which was to get Angela home without going to prison.

They would have to eat and take care of the necessities of travel, but he knew that for now they couldn't be seen together in any restaurant. That meant that they would both have to live in the tractor for the next couple of days. "Angela, why don't you come up here so we can talk things over about how we are going to get you back to your grandparents' farm? Besides, I am getting hungry, and we need to talk about that as well". Angela crawled into the seat beside him and sat looking in his direction.

"Ben, are we breaking the law? I mean, have we done something wrong? I know it was wrong of me to run away, but was it wrong of you and Abraham to help me? If it was, I guess I don't understand anything that I have heard about one person helping the other".

Ben smiled at the little girl knowing full well that she couldn't see him. "Well, Angela, I guess that would be all in the way folks look at what we have done. You were wrong to run away from your grandparents, but then again kids have been doing that for as long as there have been kids. So no, you didn't break any laws. As for me picking you up and trying to help you? We know that I didn't mean to do anything but good for you by trying to help you find your Aunt Mazie. Other folks though, might see that a bit different. So, I guess it really doesn't matter what they think as long as you and me know the truth of the matter, so I don't think you should worry about that. Okay? And did I just hear your stomach growl, or is there some kind of angry animal in this truck with us"?

Angela laughed. "That was me, alright. Grandpa always said I had a hollow leg to store my food in because my stomach was too small. I am hungry, alright".

Ben thought now was as good a time as any to tell Angela of their predicament. Things would have to be done a bit differently from now on if he was to get her safely back home to Rockville, Indiana.

"Angela, we need to have us a little talk. We have a ways to go before I can get you back to your grandparents' house, and I believe the police may be looking for me".

"You mean because you are helping me? That doesn't seem right at all, Benjamin. All you have done is try and find my Aunt Mazie for me. Even when we found out she was in heaven you tried to help me. Don't you worry, Benjamin, if the police stop you I will tell them I know Sheriff Wilson, and that if they bother you he will get after them. He is a very nice man and will see that no one does anything to you. So don't worry, Benjamin, we will be just fine".

Ben smiled at the girl's innocence and decided to let the talk go, at least for now. "Tell you what Angela, I'll stop at the first place I can find and pick us up something to fill that hollow leg of yours. We will have to eat in the truck though because we have a long way to go before tomorrow".

"That will be fine, but I do have to go to the bathroom, too. Can we stop somewhere so I can do that"?

This was something the big man hadn't counted on, and it frankly scared him a bit. There were sure to be folks that would notice a small girl riding with this huge trucker, and it would most certainly arouse suspicion. Well he thought. "That is just something we will have to deal with when the time comes. One good thing though, we are in Canada now and it may just be that no one is looking for us here".

The sun was now coming up behind them, chasing away the shadows of night. Ben wondered what Angela's reaction would be if she was ever able to see these sunrises. Or what his would be if he ever lost his sight. He would have the memories though so it wouldn't be the same. Then again, not to have ever seen a sunrise or sunset at all would just leave more excitement at the sight of them when God called her to heaven. What a glorious time that would be.

Spotting a wayside up ahead, he began gearing the big tractor down, and pulled off out of the way of any traffic that might come along. "Angela, we are at a place where you can go to the bathroom. Now, it is important that we don't make people think that you are scared or anything like that. So please hold my hand while we walk to the restrooms. There are folks about, and I don't want us to have any trouble. Is that okay with you"?

Angela smiled at the big man and opened her door. "Uncle Benjamin that will be just fine. Would you please come and help this little blind girl down"?

Ben walked around the tractor and helped her down. Holding hands, they walked to the restrooms. They were on their way back to the truck when a man's voice froze Ben in his tracks. "Hold on mister, I need to talk to you".

Still holding Angela's hand, he took a deep breath to calm himself and turned to face the man. "Benjamin, you're squeezing my hand too hard. It hurts".

The man coming toward him was holding a map and smiling. Releasing his grip on Angela's hand Ben breathed a sigh of relief and managed a smile. "Yes sir, what can I do for you"?

Looking at Angela holding the big man's hand, he smiled in return. "You folks headed someplace special are you? And who might this little one here be"?

Ben's pulse increased by tenfold and the air caught in his throat. His mind was racing trying to find an answer that would ward off any suspicion the man might have, but he could think of nothing. "My name is Angela, and this is my Uncle Ben. He has promised for a very long time to take me on one of his trips when he came to Canada, and we are having a wonderful time. We are going to the city to pick up a trailer before we head home. As you can see I am blind, but I love the smells of the countryside. Uncle Benjamin explains how things look as we drive along. It is very exciting for me". Ben nodded his agreement, and smiled.

"How very nice of you, sir. I was wondering if you knew how far it might be to the border from here. We are headed for New York City and were wondering if it would be possible to make the border before nightfall"?

"That's quite a drive from here, mister. Might be best if you planned to lay over somewhere between here and there. At night around these parts there are quite a few animals that tend to get on the road after dark, and to hit one would put you folks out of commission for some time. Could be anything from a bear to a small deer. Anything would put your vehicle out of commission though. Best to lay over like I said".

The man shook hands with Ben and was on his way. Angela pulled him down so she could whisper in his ear. "How'd I do, Benjamin"?

He picked her up and draped her over his shoulder. "Sis, no wonder you have got me running all over the country. Why, you're just about the best storyteller I've ever seen. Suppose you and me go find us a restaurant somewhere and get something to eat"?

It was twenty miles or more before they were able to find hot food. A couple of burgers, fries and a drink was about all there was right now, but Angela loved it, as all kids do. After eating, she curled up on the back bunk and was asleep in no time.

Heaven Bound pulled in to a truck stop to take on fuel. When Ben went inside to pay, an announcement on the television caught his attention. All he heard was, "The truck seems to be bob tail and has something about Heaven painted on the front somewhere". Paying for the fuel, he walked as quickly as he could without drawing attention to himself. He fired Heaven Bound's big diesel up and once again headed west toward the highway that would start them south toward Indiana and home.

Twenty

He was glad to see the sun begin to hide itself behind the horizon. He switched on the lights and settled in for what he knew would be a very long night's drive. It was sometime after midnight when the crackle of his radio made him jump. "Hey, that you up there pard"?

Ben smiled and reached for the mike. "Reckon so, what you doing here anyway? Thought you had a load to pick up somewhere"?

"Uh huh, I've had the hammer down for three hundred miles trying to catch you. Pull that monster off the road, we need to talk".

Ben pulled over the first chance he had, and he and Angela sat waiting for Abraham to come up. The passenger door opened and Abraham found himself suddenly being hugged by a very, excited twelve-year-old blind girl. "Abraham, it's good to see you. I'm glad you came back to us". Angela said, kissing the driver on the cheek. "Eeeek, Abraham, you need to shave".

Abraham sat her back up on the seat and climbed in after her. Taking his hat off, he threw it on the dash and looked at his old friend. "You heard the news"?

"Yep"

"No, you big oaf! I want to know if you have heard the news! You're a dead man, you know that? Here you are out here with a little twelve-year-old blind kid and besides that you have taken her across international borders! Man, you are clear out of your mind! What are you gonna do Benjamin? I, Abraham, your best friend in the whole world wants to know what you are gonna do"?

Ben sat looking at his friend, and it was very plain that he was very agitated right now. "You're a might worked up ain't you, Abe? I thought you said that this wasn't none of your concern anymore. Yet, here you are. What's going on, Abe"?

Abe exploded making Angela jump. "What's going on? What's going on! Man, get yourself out of this truck. I am going to knock some sense into that thick head of yours if it takes the rest of the night".

Ben smiled and said, "You're kidding, right"?

"Man, you got to do something. The whole country is looking for you two right now. Like it or not, nobody in their right mind will believe the story you will have to tell. You know that, and so do I. At the very least you are facing prison. What is the matter with you anyway? You are always doing this kind of thing. If this was the first time it might not be so bad, but it ain't. What are you, the Good Samaritan? First it was that old man you found in the ditch in where was it, Kansas? Then it was that prize bull you found standing in the road in Arkansas. You almost got yourself hung over that one. You have got to stop this, Ben, it's just plain too hard on my nerves".

"Can't help it, Abe. There are just some things that need doin, and that's that. We are about fifteen miles from the cutoff that will take us straight south into Indiana and to Angela's grandparents' farm. I ain't stopping 'til we get there. You can take the back door or the front door if you want to help. I would appreciate that, but I'm going on and taking her home. If you don't want to help you need to move on and let us be on our way".

Angela spoke up for the first time. "Benjamin, I have an idea. Why don't we just call my grandpa and have him come and get me? That way no one will know where I have been, and you and Abraham can go on and do your trucking business".

Abraham clapped his hands and looked to the heavens. "Praise be, out of the mouths of babes. There it is, Ben, that's the answer. Find a phone and get it done. Nobody will be the wiser".

"Can't do that Angela. It ain't right. I am taking you all the way home. Don't you worry, everything will be alright".

Abraham got out and slammed the door. "I ain't never seen nobody as stubborn as you. I'll take the front door. At least that way if we get red lighted or the shooting starts I can just drive away. Or at the very least say I don't know you".

Ben smiled and brought the big diesel to life. "Buckle up, Angela, we're going home".

She reached over and patted his arm. "I'm glad, Benjamin. It has been a very long ride. If you don't mind, I think I'll climb in the back and take a nap. I am very tired from all the driving".

"Don't mind at all, sis. You sleep as long as you want, should be near home when you wake up".

The soft kiss on his cheek startled him a bit, but it made him smile nonetheless. "You have been a good friend, Benjamin. I like you very much". He said nothing, but the tears on his cheeks felt cool in the night air.

Twenty-one

There is nothing quite like the sound of a big diesel when she is winding up. A quick shift, a puff of black smoke and she moves ever faster cradled in a higher gear. Those who drive these big rigs are just as determined as the rigs themselves. Men and women that have chosen the open road as their office or sometimes their homes. If you find yourself in trouble on the road they will always be there to help. More than one life has been saved by the quick thinking and quick action of the professional trucker. Be they drivers for hire or owner operators of their own rigs, they have earned and deserve respect for all that they do. Heaven Bound rocked on into the night like she had a mind of her own. Clearance lights blazed a line south and she got a thumbs up from those other night haulers she passed. Her radio would crackle once in a while and the usual line would come across. "Can't make no money runnin' bob there mister. Or "Hey, mister, looks like you lost your tagalong". The answer was always the same. "Already got me a precious cargo. Heaven Bound is working tonight. See you on down the line".

Angela woke about daylight and stretched. Climbing into the passenger seat, she buckled herself in and wanted to know where they were.

Ben looked over at her and smiled to himself. "Young lady, you are truly a mess. You know that"? Reaching into the console he produced a hairbrush and handed it to her. "Tell you what, you get yourself straightened up a bit, and I'll give you some breakfast and we will talk about where we are. How's that sound"?

She smiled back at him and took the brush. "Well, Mr. Benjamin Actually, that just sounds fine to me".

Producing two apples from the pocket on the door he handed her one and waited while she brushed her hair. Finishing, she picked up the apple and asked. "Okay, where are we? Are we close to home? And what are all the sirens about"?

"Hey sis, that's three questions at once. We are headed south on U.S. 41 and are now about fifteen miles out of your hometown of Rockville, Indiana. As for the sirens, well they have been with us now for about the last fifty miles. Two police cars in back and two in front, or there was, until this nice sheriff named Wilson came on the radio and asked if he might just pull in line directly in front of old Heaven Bound. Waved when he came around, seemed nice enough to me. Though he seemed to have a worried look on his face. He seemed to calm down a bit and waved again when you climbed over the seat just now".

Ben slowed a bit and made the turn onto U.S. 36 headed east. The Leslie farm was between Rockville and the Stringtown Road. The sirens alerted Angela's grandparents and when the procession pulled into the drive, they were waiting on the porch. Ben pulled the big tractor almost up to the porch before shutting down the diesel. Angela climbed onto his lap and together they opened the door and stepped down. There was a half circle of deputies with guns drawn and at the ready. "Put 'em away boys, this man ain't going nowhere". Lowering their guns the men remained where they were.

Grandmother Leslie came over and took Angela out of Ben's arms. "Are you alright dear? We have been so worried. You have been gone such a long time".

"Oh yes, grandmother, I am fine. I was running away and was standing out in the road. Benjamin picked me up so I wouldn't get run over by the traffic. I'm afraid I fibbed to him and told him I was on my way to see Aunt Mazie, and he was nice enough to drive me all the way to New York to see her. I think he was so nice because he knew I am blind. He and his friend Abraham, that is the one driving the big truck that was just in front of us, saved me from a very bad man in New York. When we found out Aunt Mazie was not alive anymore he brought me home".

Sheriff Wilson broke in, "Wait a minute, Angela, there was no other truck but the one you were in. Are you sure there was another truck dear"?

"Oh yes, Mr. Wilson, he was right in front of us. All of you were right between Abraham and us all the time. Surely you must have seen him"?

The sheriff made a gesture and two police cars sped out of the drive headed west on U.S. 36 with sirens blaring. Sheriff Wilson then turned to Ben. "Mister it looks like you were taken in by this little girl here. Can't say as I like the way you done things, but under the circumstances I am not at all sure you have broken any laws. Tell you what, you leave the name of the outfit you haul for with my deputy here, and you can be on your way".

Ben thanked the sheriff and handed his deputy a wrinkled card that he put into the case envelope they had built over the last few days.

Benjamin climbed into Heaven Bound and once again brought the big diesel to life. After making a circle through the yard, he drove down the drive and headed east toward Indianapolis.

Sheriff Wilson turned back to Angela, who was now in the arms of her grandfather. "Say Angela, where did that black man say he was from anyway"?

Looking up at Grandfather Leslie, she asked. "What's a black man, grandfather"?

The sheriff turned to his deputy. "Johnson, look at that card. Who does he drive for anyway? Might just send him a letter of commendation".

The deputy pulled out the card, looked at it and handed it to the sheriff. He looked at the card and put it in his shirt pocket. He ran to his car and with sirens wailing, raced down the drive and onto U.S. 36 after Heaven Bound.

Someone asked, "What the devil was that all about Johnson? What did the card say anyway"?

Johnson smiled, "God, the card said, God".

Sheriff Wilson made the five or six miles to U.S. 231 in record time. Knowing that if Heaven Bound had been in front of him he would have caught up with him, he slowed and reached for his mike. "Breaker nineteen, anyone seen a big tractor running bobtail named Heaven Bound? Got some important business".

"I gotcha nineteen. This is Sundowner, I been runnin these roads for over twenty years and if there was ever a truck named Heaven Bound, I would have heard of him by now. I know pretty much everybody out here, at least in this part of the country and there ain't no truck named Heaven Bound out here. Better check that name again".

Sheriff Wilson pulled over and turned off the engine of his cruiser and got out. He thought he heard the shifting of gears from a big rig, but it seemed to be above him. Looking up he saw nothing but a puff of black smoke, but there was no mistaking that long, lonely blast of the air horns and that big diesel humming toward home. Roll on big wheels, roll on.

End.